A Place
for Peter

Elizabeth Yates

Illustrated by Nora S. Unwin

journeyforth®

Greenville, South Carolina

Library of Congress Cataloging-in-Publication Data

Yates, Elizabeth, 1905—
A place for Peter / by Elizabeth Yates ; illustrations by Nora S.
Unwin.
p.cm.
Summary: Thirteen-year-old Peter gets a chance to earn his
doubting father's trust when he successfully handles the impor-
tant task of tapping the sugar maples to make syrup for their
mountain farm.
ISBN 0-89084-748-7
[1.Farm life—Fiction.2.Maple syrup—Fiction.3.Fathers and
sons—Fiction.4.Self-confidence—Fiction.] I.Unwin, Nora
Spicer, 1907- ill. II. Title.
PZ7.Y213Pl1994
[Fic]—dc20
94-9147
CIP
AC

A Place for Peter

Edited by Manda Cooper
Cover by Nathan Hutcheon
Line drawings by Nora S. Unwin

©1952 Coward-McCann, Inc.
©1994 BJU Press
Greenville, South Carolina 29609
JourneyForth Books is a division of BJU Press.

Printed in the United States of America

ISBN 978-0-89084-748-0
eISBN 978-1-60682-428-3

15 14 13 12 11 10 9 8 7

FOR MY FATHER

Whose own love of the land gave me the background for much that I hold most dear

Contents

JourneyForth Books by Elizabeth Yates
Carolina's Courage
Sound Friendships
The Next Fine Day
Sarah Whitcher's Story
Someday You'll Write
The Seventh One

JourneyForth Sets by Elizabeth Yates
Mountain Born
A Place for Peter

The Journeyman
Hue & Cry

Swiss Holiday
Iceland Adventure
American Haven

1 Too Young

Martha looked from the kitchen window, watching Andrew and Peter cross the space that separated the house from the barn. Peter had grown tall this past year. Now, at thirteen, he stood shoulder-high to his father, but he was lean and rangy and had nothing of Andrew's muscular build. Martha sighed as she watched them. They were standing outside the barn, and Andrew was shaking his head.

Something must have gone wrong between them, Martha thought. She shook her head too, for it seemed that with every passing month, and with every inch Peter added to his height, he grew further away from his father. Once there had been such understanding between them; now it seemed there was little upon which they could agree.

Peter humped his shoulders and turned away, dragging his feet over the snow in reluctant obedience to some word of his father's.

"The mail!" Martha exclaimed. Why was it Peter so consistently forgot to go the short distance down the lane to where it met the road and their mailbox stood? It seemed such a small task his father expected him to do, yet Peter was so forgetful of it. Martha felt she could sympathize with Andrew's annoyance, yet her heart went out to her son. "Andrew won't let him grow up," she said to herself. "He won't give Peter tasks that are worthy of him."

It was time for the milking, and Peter wanted to be in the barn helping his father. Martha sighed again. Often there was nothing in the box at all, and sometimes just their farm paper. It did not seem important to Peter to go for the mail. That was why he forgot it.

Martha turned back to her work, thinking to herself that the year was well on its way out of winter and into spring, for the sun even at its setting was warm, and the shadows it cast on the snow were long and strong. It would be time for supper soon and her menfolk would be hungry. Opening the door of the iron stove, she put in more wood. The dry chunks of birch and maple crackled and leaped swiftly into flame. Martha closed the door slowly, letting herself sniff with delight the first fragrance of the wood. She pushed the kettle over the heat and felt as if she were no longer alone in the kitchen when the kettle began to sing.

She took some potatoes from the bin to peel for their supper, then glanced out the window once more to see if the first star had come. Of the things that marked her day, that first star on the edge of evening was one she loved and looked for. But the sky was still pale with light. It was too early for the star. Her wish would have to wait. She saw Peter turn from the lane toward the house with something white in his hand.

There was a flutter of excitement in her heart. It could only be for her! Had it been a letter for his father, Peter would have carried it to the barn.

Peter came into the kitchen and put the letter on the table.

"You left it in the box a long time," Martha said quietly.

Peter thrust his mittens into his pocket and held his hands to the stove. "Most of the time there's nothing there," he answered.

"It's best to go when your father expects you to. You never know when there might be something important."

"Nothing important happens up here," Peter muttered. "We live so far away from everything."

"Oh, Peter," Martha said, looking at him in surprise, "life is where we live, how we live. You wouldn't find it very different if you were down in the village, or even far away in a big city."

He made no reply.

"Peter, try to remember to go for the mail first thing in the afternoon. It's what your father wants you to do."

"I was going for it in a minute. He didn't have to tell me." Peter took his warmed hands away from the stove and looked quickly at his mother. "He doesn't always have to tell me, as if I were too young to be trusted."

"Peter, Peter." Martha saw his flushed cheeks, his eyes bright and rebellious. Whatever words he'd had with his father were still rankling. She held out her arms, but the gesture was a futile one, for Peter turned and left the room, whistling to himself.

Martha sat down at the table and picked up the knife to start paring the potatoes. She did not understand this new Peter, this boy who was growing away from both of them. No, perhaps she did not understand him any more than Andrew did. Then she remembered the letter. Putting her knife down, she reached across the table for it and drew it to her.

She stared at the envelope. It was her brother Kenneth's writing. He had written her once a year since she had left her home to marry Andrew and live in mountain country. She had received his annual letter at Christmas time. Why was he writing her again so soon, and this—her eyes strayed from the letter to the calendar on the wall—and this only the first week in March? She opened the letter and read it slowly, a heaviness in her heart. Things out of their time often bore no good.

The clock ticked on. The kettle sang. The first faint approach of twilight came into the room, but Martha sat with the letter in her hands, the paring knife beside her and the potatoes still in their jackets.

"Leonard," she kept saying over and over to herself, "Leonard, you must live."

4

Leonard was the youngest of her brothers and the one who had always had a little more of her heart than the others. She saw him still as a boy, bringing in the cows from pasture, riding on the loads of hay. She had not seen him since he had become a man, but she knew what he was like. Tall and strong and smiling, a farmer to the bone and a newly married man. When was it he had said in his last letter that the baby was due? Martha glanced again at the calendar. June, he had said. If he were disabled for long, his young wife might not be able to give him all the help he might need.

"Oh, Leonard, wait for me. I'll come. I'll take care of you."

She looked up at the clock. Had she known of the accident sooner she might have been able to get a train that afternoon. But how could she leave Andrew and Peter and the work of the farm? She looked down at the letter in her hands, shaking her head slowly. Aware, now, that it was almost too dark to see the words on the page, she folded it into the envelope and put it in the pocket of her apron.

Realizing that she had been letting time slide through idle fingers, she rose quickly from the table to fetch a lamp. Passing the window, she paused. There was her star, poised over the barn roof, shining out of the darkness into her heart. She smiled at it and made her wish: a different one than she might have made had she seen it earlier.

She lit the lamp and began her preparation for supper, moving quickly, singing to herself as she went around the kitchen. Footsteps could be heard outside and then the door opened. Andrew and Peter came into the room with the dog, Shepherdess. Andrew was carrying a pail of milk which he set down near the window. Peter had a basket of eggs which he placed on the table.

"Supper will be ready soon, Andrew, almost as soon as you and Peter are ready for it."

Andrew sat down heavily. A long weary sigh escaped him as he bent over to unlace his boots. His house shoes were warming behind the stove. Peter brought them to him, then went upstairs to his own room.

"Don't get reading and forget to come down to eat," Andrew called after him.

Martha laughed. "A boy doesn't forget his stomach, Andrew. Seems as if you should know that."

Andrew made no response.

Martha crossed the kitchen with a bowl of food in her hand for Shep. Passing beside Andrew, she laid her free hand on his shoulder. "Don't take your tiredness out on the boy," she said.

Andrew glanced up at her, a look of puzzlement on his face. "I'll try not to, but he does forget, Martha, so much, so often. Sometimes I wonder he doesn't forget his name."

"He's got a lot on his mind," Martha said as she set Shep's bowl on the floor and drew her hand over the dog's long coat.

Shep looked up and wagged her tail, as much in response to the knowing hand as at the prospect of the food.

"On his mind!" Andrew echoed, laughing harshly.

"Can't you remember, Andrew," Martha said, "what it was like when you were his age? I can—everyone giving you orders but no one really trusting you; so many things to remember, yet when you forgot, you were unable to explain why. Sometimes I think all that Peter needs is to be trusted more and told less."

Andrew looked at her questioningly.

"Oh," Martha smiled swiftly, "I've been remembering a lot this afternoon. That's why I'm late with supper."

Andrew went over to the sink to wash. "Peter said you had a letter."

"Yes. From Kenneth. It's about Leonard. I'll tell you about it after supper."

Something in Martha's voice disturbed Andrew. He turned toward her quickly. "Is Leonard all right?"

Martha shook her head.

Andrew dried his hands and crossed the kitchen to stand beside her. "I'm sorry, Martha. He was always your favorite, wasn't he?"

"He *is* my favorite," Martha answered stoutly; then she went toward the stove. "I'll tell you later. Not now. Not at supper. Call Peter," she said. "I'll put things on the table."

After supper, Andrew asked Peter to go out to the barn to make the rounds and close the door for the night. Peter looked at his father in amazement. Never before had he been given this final task of the day.

"See that Princess has enough hay. She's growing so, she needs more than the others."

"I will, Father." Peter started to put his coat on. "Don't you want me to help Mother with the dishes first?"

"I'm helping her tonight."

"Come on, Shep," Peter called.

Obediently Shep left her warm place behind the stove and followed Peter. She was slow in all her movements now, and a rush of cold air came into the room as Peter held the door for her.

"She'll have her puppies soon," Andrew commented, his practiced eye knowing that the new life that made her body heavy was not many days from being born.

While they did the dishes, Martha told Andrew of the letter she had received that afternoon. "It was an accident while they were cutting ice. Leonard was badly hurt. His ribs were crushed. Kenneth says he keeps asking for me. He says—" Martha paused.

Andrew put down the dishtowel and laid his hand on Martha's shoulder.

The gesture gave Martha strength. She looked at him. Her eyes were full of tears but her voice was steady. "He says they don't know how long Leonard can live. What shall I do, Andrew?"

"I think you must go to them," Andrew said briefly. It was not an answer he gave easily, but it was the only one he could give.

"It's hard to be needed in two places," Martha said, "in your own home and in the home of your childhood."

"It may not be for so long," Andrew said comfortingly.

"It may be for longer than any of us thinks," Martha replied practically.

"Peter and I can make out."

"And Shep?" Martha had so wanted to be with Shep when the dog brought her first puppies into the world.

"Shep will be all right." Andrew smiled at Martha's concern. "More young things than puppies have come to birth on this farm."

"There's a train tomorrow morning at ten o'clock."

"Yes," Andrew said with a nod. "You must take it. If you do, you'll be there by evening."

Peter came in from the barn, glowing from the frosty night. He hung up his coat and cap, kicked off his boots, and stood by the stove. Shep nudged against him as she sought her special retreat back of the stove, lowering her body carefully, pushing her nose between her forepaws, and closing her eyes.

"Your mother is going away, Peter," Andrew said. "There was bad news in that letter. She is needed in her home."

"Mother?" Peter looked at Martha. Anything else he might have said seemed to choke in his throat.

"Come up to bed, Peter. I'll tell you about it when we are upstairs. Uncle Leonard has been hurt. They want me to help nurse him back to health. I shall leave tomorrow morning. I won't be away more than a few weeks."

She started from the room.

Peter followed her. Too stunned by the news to say anything, he did not remember to call good night to his father until he had reached the top of the stairs.

Andrew heard their voices in the room above him. The sharp questioning tone of Peter's, the smooth tone of Martha's. Then there was a silence, and after the silence he heard Martha's voice, steady now, and even. She was reading to Peter. She would continue until he was asleep, or so near sleep that she knew she could leave him in peace. Andrew smiled. Though he heard no words, the sound of the voice brought composure to him too.

Half an hour later Martha returned to the kitchen to sit at the table with a basket of mending.

Andrew looked up from his accounts book. "Had Peter given you that letter sooner, you might be already on your way."

"He knows that, Andrew, but what gain can come to any of us if Peter reproaches himself half the night?"

Andrew turned back to his book. Then he said without looking up, "You must have many things to do this evening."

"All in good time," Martha replied. "There are some socks that need mending first."

Andrew closed his book and put his head in his hands, something between a sigh and a groan escaping him.

"Is it the same thing?" Martha asked quietly.

"Always the same," he answered. "For two years now the market for wool has been off, and that for mutton is no better."

"But the cows are doing well, aren't they?"

He shook his head. "Not until the herd is increased will we ever see any profit from them. Expenses mount and there is little return. Peter is small help to me and Benj is so old." Andrew ran his hands through his hair. "I don't know what will happen to us all unless there's a change for the better soon."

Martha put down her mending and looked across the table at her husband—the troubled brow, the brooding eyes, the lines that care had dug down his face, the strong hands. There was so little she could say when Andrew saw just the sorry side of their affairs. There were things of which she was sure—the mountains around them, the creatures of the farm, the land with its yield and increase, Peter growing to share his father's problems. Such things must be real to Andrew too, yet after his days of hard work and a market of falling prices, even Martha found it hard to remind him of what she knew was good and constant in their lives.

"I won't go, Andrew. I think you need me more than Leonard."

He dropped his hands and looked at her quickly. "No, you must go. I'm sorry, Martha. I'll be all right."

"You and Peter," she reminded him. To herself she said, "And the land in which you both are rooted."

Next morning Martha was in the kitchen early getting breakfast when a knock sounded at the door.

"Come in," she called, wondering what neighbor could be abroad at such an hour.

It was Mary, Peter's friend from down in the valley. She hurried into the kitchen. "Oh, Aunt Martha," she cried, "Granny heard from her cousin that your brother had met with an accident. She wondered if you would be going away, and she sent me up to see if I could do anything to help you." Mary flung her arms around Martha in a rush of feeling.

Martha held the girl close to her for a moment. Then she held her off at arm's length and looked deep into the clear young face. There was no tie that bound them save that of the heart, but it was strong. Mary lived in the village in the valley with her grandmother, but she had always called Martha and Andrew "aunt" and "uncle." Peter was like a brother to her, and she regarded the farm on the hill as a second home.

"Shall you be gone long?"

"I don't know. When there's illness, it's hard to tell how long it may last."

"Gran said to tell you that she would be glad to come up every week and give the house a good cleaning. I'll come with her too."

"You are kind, Mary, you and your grandmother, but the men should be able to keep things fairly tidy. I hope I won't be away long." Martha had not meant to sigh, but she did and Mary caught the unmistakable sound of a troubled heart.

"I'm sorry, Aunt Martha. Was the news so bad?"

"It's not that. That's something I can take hold of when I come to it. It's my menfolk here that set me to worrying."

"But Peter—" Mary began, "but Uncle Andrew—" Her words hung questioning on the air.

"It's nothing to bother you about, Mary. It's just that there seems to be so little understanding between the two of them."

"Can't Benj help?"

"Benj is busy with the sheep. He takes care of them while Peter helps his father with the cows and the chickens. Benj stays at his own house now most of the time."

"But Peter could go over to see Benj," Mary suggested hopefully.

"He could," Martha agreed. Then, hearing Peter's steps on the stairs, her tone changed abruptly. "They'll be all right, Mary."

"Hello, Mary," Peter said. "You're around early."

"Hello, Peter."

Andrew came in from the barn, carrying a pail of milk. He smiled at Mary. "You've heard that Martha is leaving us?"

"Yes, I came up to see if I could help."

"Mary's going to have breakfast with us," Martha said, setting a fourth place at the table. "We can leave her at her house when you take me to the train. Mary, your grandmother won't mind if we keep you, will she?"

"She'll think you've found something for me to do." Mary laughed.

"Perhaps we have," Martha said as she greased the griddle with salt pork and poured out the first batch of pancakes. While waiting for them to brown, she turned some strips of bacon in the frying pan.

It was as if Martha were not going away. There was much gaiety as they sat around the breakfast table with pancakes disappearing almost as soon as they were made, and Andrew smiling like his old self as he told Mary about Buttercup Princess, the youngest of his heifers and the one in whom he took such pride. Martha went often to the stove to make new pancakes, returning to the table with the platter piled high.

When the last drop had been drained from the jug of syrup, Andrew said, "That's the end of the syrup. There'll be no more till we boil down this year's sap."

"That will be soon, won't it?" Mary asked.

"Soon now," Andrew replied. "This strong March sun will draw the sap up the trees and we'll get a fine flow, won't we, Martha?"

"You will," Martha said.

Andrew looked at her questioningly, then his expression changed. He had forgotten for the moment that she was going away. Now the fact jabbed sharply into his mind. For years past, Martha had done the boiling down with only occasional help from himself or Benj. How could there be any syrup this year without Martha? Andrew wanted to protest. He wanted to say, "You can't go now! We can't spare you!" but he knew it was no use. There were endless reasons that Martha should not leave the farm; yet the one demand that she go to her own home in time of need dwarfed all the reasons.

Andrew looked down at his plate. "Perhaps we won't have any syrup this year."

Peter felt bold. "I could do it, Father! I've been with Mother ever so often when she's done the boiling. I'm sure I could do it myself." He looked eagerly at his father.

Andrew shook his head. "I can't spare Benj to help you, and it wouldn't be possible for you to do it all by yourself."

Breakfast was soon over and the dishes were quickly done. Then Mary went to the barn with Andrew. Peter stood by the kitchen table, waiting for the moment when his mother would say good-by. This was a new moment in his life and he felt bewildered by it. He had left the farm for a day or so at a time—going up to the hills with Benj when the sheep were put on summer grazing, going down to the valley to do some work for Mary's grandmother—but never had his mother left him. Seeing her standing there with her hat and coat on gave him a strange feeling, as if part of the house were going off and, once it went, the winds that would tear about him would be cold and fearful.

"How soon will you be back?"

"I don't know, Peter. I'll come as soon as I can."

"Do you—do you have to go?"

Martha sighed. "I wouldn't be leaving the farm, Peter, if the need there weren't greater than it is here."

Peter knew that. He shouldn't have said what he did. Even he could see that such words only made it harder for his mother.

"Peter," Martha said quietly, "come here."

Slowly Peter crossed the kitchen to stand in front of his mother.

"Peter, try not to do anything to vex your father."

Peter looked away. How could he ever tell his mother that he did not mean to vex his father, that he did not mean to forget to do things? He swallowed hard.

"Peter." Martha compelled him to look at her. "Your father has had many worries this last year, more even than he has told me. The market for wool has been off and the sheep have not done what he expects them to do to keep the farm going, but he has great hopes for the cows. With another heifer or two to assure him a good herd, he'll be a happier man. Be patient with him until then. It wasn't easy for him to lose Cynthia Queen last winter."

"It wasn't easy for me either," Peter mumbled. Queen was the only one of his father's cows that he had ever felt any real affection for.

"I know, Peter, but with you it was just your heart; with your father it was his heart and his pocketbook, and that comes hard to a farmer. He'll breed Buttercup Princess when she's ready, but it takes time to build a herd."

"Yes, I realize that."

"Try to understand your father, Peter, for you'll never know a man until you know some of the tribulations he endures. He has been carrying a far heavier load than either you or I can imagine. Remember that, when he seems hard with you."

"I could help him more if he'd let me."

"He will, Peter, when he trusts you."

"He'll never trust me."

"Never is a long time, Peter, and none of us lives to see its length."

Peter was silent for a moment. Then he said slowly, "I wish he would trust me with something big."

"He will, when you are worthy." Martha smiled confidently at her son. "And the only way we can prove ourselves worthy of a big trust is by doing well the tasks that belong to each day."

"Yes, but—" Peter began.

"Sometimes there aren't any buts, Peter. If we accept what is our life, we grow through it and because of it. That's the way we grow up."

Martha put her hand on Peter's shoulder. Going away like this just at the spring of the year, just when life was starting on the farm, was hard; but it might prove to be the best thing for Peter. She had been the bridge between him and Andrew long enough. They would have to learn to meet each other now, each in his own way.

"I can't say any more, Peter," Martha said as she put her arms around him and embraced him.

Peter's voice sounded muffled. "I think I know what you mean, Mother. I'll do my best to help Father. I promise you I will."

Releasing him, Martha smiled at him. "I hope you'll get up to the sugar bush soon. The world will look different to you from up there. It always does to me."

Peter nodded. "I shall, Mother. The week after next there's no school and that ought to be a good time for the sap, if the spring doesn't come on too fast."

The mere thought of doing something that might win his mother's approval buoyed Peter. He returned her smile with a broad one of his own. "Don't worry about anything here," he assured her. "Father and I can take care of this farm, and the sheep are always all right with Benj. I'll write you; every week I'll write you. It will just be about the things you know—"

"Oh, but that's what I'll want to hear!"

Andrew came into the room. "Time to go, Martha. Mary's waiting in the truck."

"All right, Andrew."

Martha took a last look around the familiar kitchen—at the oxalis in the window, a mass of pink blossoms. Beyond, across the snowy fields, stood the mountains, silent in farewell as in all else. Strong, pine-girt ramparts, they would look down on her world, making it a haven until her return. She brought her gaze back to the kitchen, to the wide table and shiny black stove, to the boy whose face was young and questioning, to the man whose face was lined with the troubles he could not share.

Well, Martha thought, whatever comes, I've given them both my best, these many years and more.

Andrew picked up the suitcase and started from the room. Martha went over to Shep and stroked the dog's silky coat. Shep's tail wagged, and gentle eyes clung with longing to the one who had meant food and understanding for so long.

"Keep the house until I get back," Andrew said to Peter.

"I will," Peter replied. "Good-by," he called after the two figures disappearing through the open door.

"Good-by," they called back.

When the door closed behind them, Peter felt encased in loneliness. How to keep a house without his mother in it, he wondered, for it was she who made it home. He went over to the stove and sat on the floor beside Shep. The ache within him was more than he could bear alone.

2 In the Sugar Bush

"Yes, of course, you can try doing the sugaring," his father said in answer to Peter's inquiry a morning or two later, "but I doubt if I can give you any help and Benj has his hands full."

"I'd like to see how much I can do on my own."

"Don't neglect your other work."

"I won't, I promise. I've done the hens already this morning so I could leave right after breakfast and go up to the sugar bush on my way to school."

His father looked pleased. So often he had to remind Peter to do the hens. "That's going a long way around to school."

"But it's quicker than the road for skis," Peter said eagerly. "There's enough snow in the fields to give me a fine run all the way down to the valley."

His father pushed back his chair from the table. Peter started to carry the dishes to the sink.

"I'll take care of everything here," Andrew said. "You'd best get on your way now."

A smile broke across Peter's face. "Can't I help you?"

"Not now. Not here. Perhaps later."

Peter let out a shout of joy and bent over to lace his boots. He buttoned his coat and pulled his cap down over his ears. At the door he turned back to face his father.

"How soon will we hear from Mother?"

"There may be a letter today."

"Father, I—I'll go to the mailbox on my way home from school, before I go up to the woods."

"All right, Peter."

"Father?"

"Yes?"

"Do you think Uncle Leonard will get better?"

Andrew nodded his head. "If he held on to life until your mother got there, she'll nurse him back to health all right."

Peter looked relieved. "Good-by, Father."

"Good-by, son."

Every morning that week Peter went to the sugar bush before he went to school; the half-hour, slim as it was and sliced in between chores and school, counted for valuable preparation toward the work he wanted to do.

The grove of sugar maples stood in the woods a quarter of an hour's walk from the house. Most of the trees were of a great age, with huge, high crowns and furrowed shaggy bark, but in and among them were seedlings and saplings and stalwart young trees. In a clearing stood a small sugar house, its roof swayed by the years that had passed over it and the snows it had borne. Its slab sides had withstood many a tempest roaring through the forest; heavy snows had piled against them, and summer suns, filtering through the grove, had dried and silvered the wood.

Inside the sugar house was a big evaporator and a storage tank that held the sap and let it into the evaporator by gravity. Against one wall stood an old iron stove that was used for cooking meals or for boiling down the sap when the flow was not heavy. This stove Peter intended to use. Working alone, he would not be able to handle the evaporator and the endless appetite for wood of the fire beneath it.

The first day he cleaned the spigots and buckets and set them in readiness on top of the storage tank; the next day he cleaned the stove and repaired the pipe so it would be ready and safe for the hot fire he would have in it; and the day after that he sawed and split wood, stacking it in convenient piles. All the time he checked on his equipment and tried to remember every step of the work that his mother had done when he had been with her.

On his way home from school Thursday afternoon, Peter went around by the sheep farm to talk with Benj. He found the old man sitting outside his small house in the warm sunshine, cleaning tools. Benj had always been old—that was Peter's memory of him since a child, but like a tree of massive trunk and wide crown, he never seemed to get any older.

"Sap's rising today, Benj!"

"It is indeed." Benj nodded, setting down a tool and looking up at the sky. "By the look of things, and the feel, we're in for a nice run of weather. Too bad your mother isn't home. She always liked the early spring days up in the sugar bush, and I liked being up there with her."

"Benj," Peter said, leaning toward him excitedly, "I'm going to do the sugaring for her."

"You are?"

"Next week there's no school. It's spring vacation. I'm going to work every day in the sugar bush, and I should have something to show for it."

"You should indeed." Benj looked more closely at Peter. "What has your father to say, for he's told me nothing of this, and I'd not planned on going up to the sugar bush at all this year?"

"He says I can give it a try," Peter replied carelessly.

Benj was silent with that way of his of looking into space, so that one watching him would find it hard to tell whether he was seeing or hearing. After a few moments he said quietly, "When do you start?"

"Tomorrow morning I'm going to tap the trees and set the buckets out. If the sap flows well, I should have enough to start boiling on Saturday."

"How many buckets do you plan on setting out?"

Peter hesitated. His mother set out two hundred, but then she had Andrew or Benj to help her with the heaviest work. Single-handed as he would be, Peter had not yet figured out how many buckets he could care for.

Benj supplied the answer. "Don't do more than you can handle easily. Thirty or forty buckets will be a good lot for a start. If I can get up to help you, perhaps we can do more."

"Oh, Benj, do you think you can?"

"We'll see," Benj said dubiously, but his eyes were twinkling.

Peter asked Benj a dozen questions, and when he started on the way home he had a feeling of confidence about the operation before him. That was like Benj, Peter thought. He always made you feel you could accomplish what you gave yourself to do.

Peter, with his skis over his shoulder, walked up the road until he came to the farm lane where the mailbox stood. As he opened it eagerly, its emptiness yawned at him. He tried to tell himself that they could not hope for a letter every day, and yesterday had brought the good news that Uncle Leonard would get better.

At the house, Peter thrust his skis in a snowbank near the door and went out to the barn to give the hens their afternoon feed of grain. He took a basket with him for the eggs. He called to the hens before he opened their door and went in among them, and they accepted him in their midst without fluttering or excitement. When he rattled the grain in the bucket under his arm, they started to gather around him, making small eager sounds. Their eyes, which had surveyed him coolly, gleamed with expectancy.

"Hi, girls," Peter said, "how are you today?"

The hens, slowly coming out of their winter molt, were anything but handsome. Unusually shy because of their loose feathers, they had adopted an apologetic attitude. Peter, in whose special care they were, gave them extra corn, hoping to hasten the growth of their new feathers. Angular movements became swift and agitated as Peter tossed the grain among them. Clucking and pecking, they ate it greedily.

Peter watched them, glad at the change that was coming over them as perceptibly as it was coming over the world. Squawker was still just a noise and a mouth, and even the feathers that were beginning to cover her could not give her any dignity; but Copper Queen was showing more russet flashes every day and soon she would be worthy of the name that had been given her when she was a proud young pullet. Amazon now had enough feathers to ruffle them like the fighting cock she thought she was. Blondie, the beautiful, walked serenely among the flock. Still as free of feathers as the trees were of leaves, she had dignity that seemed independent of outer covering. She looked up at Peter, making a curious clucking sound of pleasure at the good taste of the corn he had given them.

Peter reached down and stroked her. "Never mind, Blondie, you'll soon be yourself again."

When Peter went to the nest to gather the eggs, he turned back reproachfully to the flock. "Only three between the dozen of you!"

The hens cocked their heads and watched him as he placed the eggs in the basket he had brought with him.

"Sap's rising," Peter informed them. "Maybe that will make you feel you ought to get busy and start laying more eggs."

He left the hen pen with that admonition. The hens followed him to the door, then stood in a silent group after he went out. They looked at each other, stretching out their necks and flapping their wings; then they went solemnly back and scratched among the shavings on the floor, searching for kernels of corn that might have eluded them.

The next morning Peter ate his breakfast quickly and prepared to leave for the sugar house as soon as he had done his chores. Shep looked longingly at him.

"No, Shep, not today," Peter said, stroking her gently.

Reluctantly the dog went back to her place behind the stove.

The sun had not long been risen from behind the mountains. Its light was brilliant across the snow and its rays were strong and heartening. Widespread in the air was a feeling that everything in nature was reaching out and up to the warmth and brilliance.

"Sap should flow today," Andrew said as he stood in the doorway and watched Peter adjust the clamps on his skis.

"I plan to tap as many of the trees as I can," Peter said. He looked up at his father longingly, wishing that Andrew were coming with him. "Father—" he began.

"Good luck to you," Andrew said.

Peter turned away quickly. Of course his father could not think of coming. He had too many things to do. Important things. He stood up and reached for his ski poles, then thrust them into the snow.

Andrew watched the boy push off across the flattened snow near the house.

"Bye," Peter shouted, waving one of his ski poles. Then, leaning to the contour of the land, he let the skis give him swift transit across the fields and up the slope toward the woods.

Once at the maple grove, Peter exchanged skis for the snowshoes he kept in the sugar house. Going from tree to tree with his brace and bit, spigots, and buckets, he worked fast to make best use of the edge of time that he had.

Bending over on the snow by one of the big trees, he bored a hole in the trunk, careful not to get near a hole made the previous year but keeping the level the same, a good four feet from the ground. It was hard work. Slowly the curled shavings of maple fell onto the snow. When Peter felt that he had gone about two and a half inches into the tree, he cleaned out the hole and drove a spigot into it; then he attached a bucket to the hook under the spigot, fixed the lid securely in place, and went on to drill another hole. Two buckets were hung on every tree, and before the hour he had allowed himself was gone, he had thirty buckets out.

In spigot after spigot the sap gathered slowly, then one drop after another slid down into the buckets. *Drip, drop. Drip, drop.* Before Peter left the grove, a gratifying symphony resounded in his ears and echoed through the stillness of the woods.

The sun felt warmer already and the snow was softening noticeably. The sap had a gentle but steady flow. Given a day, the buckets might have a fair quantity in them before Peter returned to the grove. Peter stooped over the last spigot and lifting the bucket away knelt down on the snow and pressed his lips to the spigot, sucking the sap as it came from the tree. It was like clear cool water with a touch of sweetening.

Peter unbuckled his snowshoes and hung them in the sugar house, then clamped on his skis and took up the poles. With one last look around the grove at the buckets hanging expectantly, with one last cocking of his ears to catch the sound of the sap dripping slowly into them, Peter turned and sped on his way through the woods and down across the open fields into the valley. He was fleet and sure, though he was almost giddy with delight at the thing he had started in the maple grove.

At school, the boys and girls were bubbling over with talk of what they were going to do during their week's vacation. At recess it was the main topic of discussion. Some were going away to visit friends or cousins; many of them would be helping their parents on their farms, and as most of the work just then was sugaring, a good deal of time would be spent in the different maple orchards up and down the valley.

Randy's father had a big maple orchard, a team of oxen for the sap gathering, and enough help to keep the boiling going day and night. Randy was proud of the part he played yearly in the sugaring, and he announced confidently that this year his father expected to make all of five hundred gallons of syrup.

"Everything's in our favor so far," he said. Then he turned to Peter. "What are you going to do this week?"

"Sugaring, just like you."

"Is your father going to help?"

"No, he hasn't got time this year."

"Benj going to help?"

Peter shook his head.

"How are you going to do it then?"

"By myself."

Randy whistled. Some of the girls looked admiringly at Peter, while one or two of the boys stared at him in open-mouthed astonishment.

"You won't get through very much alone," Randy announced in a superior way.

"Maybe I'll boil down more than you think," Peter replied, feeling jaunty before his friends.

"When are you starting?" Randy asked.

"Starting?" Peter grinned, for now he was the superior one. "I've started. Got things going this morning. Sap's running just as nice as you please into the buckets I set out."

Randy whistled again. "Spry is your middle name," he said; then he clapped Peter on the shoulder. "I'm coming up some day to test your product."

"Come along!"

Mary said, "Maybe we'll all come up to taste your syrup, Peter."

"If you do," Peter warned, "I'll find work for every one of you."

They laughed. Some of them said they wouldn't come then, for work wasn't what vacation was for; but there was not one of them who didn't envy Peter the adventure before him. Master of his own sugar grove as he was that year, any boy in the school would have been willing to change places with him, and not a few of the girls.

The bell rang and they went trooping back to the schoolhouse. No one carried his head higher than Peter, and so full of plans was it that he found it hard to keep his mind on his books.

That night, after Peter and Andrew ate the last of the food Martha had left for them, Peter told his father that he would like to spend the whole of the next day at the sugar bush.

"All right," his father said. "You've got the weather with you, Peter. That sunset tonight means another day just like this—warm sun as long as it's in the sky and a drop below freezing at nightfall."

"Can't you come up sometime during the day?" Peter asked hopefully.

Andrew shook his head. "I'm going over to Green Mead Farm to see a bull I want to breed Buttercup Princess with. That's a day's journey."

"Will you be back for the milking?"

"Yes, I'll be back in time for that. You won't need to leave your work until you've finished for the day."

Peter started up the stairs. Halfway up he paused. "Father?"

Andrew looked up from his farm paper.

"Couldn't I take Shep with me?"

"No," Andrew said; then he shook his head. "I'm afraid you've set yourself a lonely task."

Peter went on up the stairs, and Andrew returned to his paper.

Shep got up from her place back of the stove. She looked over at Andrew, but no word or flicking finger demanded anything of her; so she went quietly up the stairs. Before Peter's closed door she raised a paw and drew it softly down the wood.

Peter heard the faint familiar sound and opened the door.

Shep went into the room. She wagged her plumy tail, then sat down on her haunches and pushed her forepaws along the floor until she could rest her nose on them. Peter sat on the floor beside her and put his arms around her, burying his head in her long coat. She rubbed her nose against him. Shep was lonely too.

Peter left early the next morning, long before the sun was up, though light was in the sky. He tied his muffler tight around his neck and pulled down the earflaps on his cap. It was as cold as any winter morning, yet the cold was only a reminder of the strength of the winter, for spring was in the air. Peter went swiftly on his skis over the crusty surface of the snow, down the pasture slope, across the frozen brook, and up the road into the woods.

A snowshoe rabbit, white as the world it inhabited, darted out from a tree stump, looked with interest at Peter, then wheeled and snapped his hind feet on the hard crust and disappeared into the woods. Standing still and leaning on his ski poles, Peter looked back at the country he had put behind him. Breathing deep breaths of the frosty air that caught in his throat, he felt like shouting with joy. This was sugar weather: a cold, cold night and a cloudless morning washed with the pale, white light of dawn.

The day was crystal clear and the whole countryside was white with its snow covering. The distant mountains stood out like stalwart walls protecting the valley that stretched away to the east and the south. Peter could see clusters of houses, and here and there a farmstead with smoke coming from a chimney. The light was intensifying behind the mountains, and he watched the sun rise in lonely splendor—tingeing the far hills with rose before the east glowed golden, suffusing the sky, touching the earth, so that the world Peter saw and knew and loved became lapped in radiance.

"Hello, sun!" he shouted, feeling that he must speak to someone.

Behind him in the woods, pheasants were calling. Nearby on a branch rang out the exultant note of a chickadee. Winging across the valley came a small flock of grosbeaks with their curious undulating flight. They alighted in a tree that had some frozen apples still hanging from its boughs. Soon they would have their fill of seeds if they could get through the wrinkled skins of the fruit. Peter took one look back at his father's farm and saw blue smoke curling from the chimney of the house, hanging for a moment in the cold air, then moving straight up to lose itself in deeper blue. It was like a hand waving, and he waved back to it.

Up at the sugar house Peter got a roaring fire going in the stove. Then he buckled on his snowshoes and went around to the trees to visit his buckets. Some had more in them than others, but all were half full in any case and solid with ice. Two by two, Peter carried them back to the sugar house and stood them near the warmth of the stove until the ice loosened and was ready to come out; then he tipped the frozen sap into the big boiling pan. The fire soon melted it, and before Peter had brought the last bucket back to the stove, the contents of the pan were already simmering.

Now before him lay the whole long stretch of time his father had warned him about. Beyond doing a few small chores, there was nothing for him to do for hours and hours but stoke the fire and wait. It was indeed a lonely task he had set himself.

Peter stood in the warm sunshine in the open doorway of the sugar house. Outside in the grove he could hear the occasional tinkle as a drop of sap gathered in a spigot and fell into a bucket; behind him was the deep rumbling of the sap as it boiled in the pan. Clouds of steam rose from the pan; sweet steam that, as the hours went on, developed more and more of a maple fragrance. Scum rose to the surface and Peter skimmed it off. Stirring the sap, he saw with satisfaction that an hour's hard boiling had reduced the level by an inch.

After he had split and stacked some wood for future fires, he cooked his luncheon, drawing on a cache of supplies he had brought previously to the sugar house; then he sat outside on an upturned sap bucket and ate his leisurely meal.

The sun was so warm that he soon took off his coat. The air that had little but silence in it during the colder part of the morning was alive with the movement of birds. A nuthatch scurried up the trunk of a maple; a downy woodpecker drilled one small hole and then another; two red squirrels played tag with each other on a maple branch high above the ground. Every now and then they called a halt in their game to cling to the limb and nibble on the sweet icicles formed by chilling winds on flowing sap. Sometimes they sucked a run of sap from a crack in the bark, and often, finding no convenient crack, they slit one for themselves. syrup

Beyond the grove, where pine and hemlock darkened the woods, Peter heard a clumsy sound. Straining his eyes to see, he spied a large black porcupine coming out of its lair in the rocks, shaking itself unconcernedly and going slowly across the snow to a hemlock. Surveying the tree for a moment, it clambered awkwardly up to find a perch among the branches from which it might feast on cones. Peter stretched back in the sun against a tree trunk, waited, and watched.

The clouds of steam were denser when next he went in to stoke the fire. He tasted the boiling sap. It had more than sweetness to it now; it had flavor—maple flavor.

He made the round of the buckets, emptying some of the full ones into the storage container in the sugar house. It was long past noon and the sun had begun to lose its warmth. The sap was flowing no more into the buckets, for the cold was drawing it down to the roots again. However, the sap in the pan was at the point where it had to be closely watched. It had boiled down to within a few inches of the bottom. Peter remembered that from then on his mother would never leave it; a moment could be too much; a moment more than was needed could darken the whole batch.

Tasting, testing, pouring some on the snow to see how it hardened, then finally plunging the thermometer in for cer- tainty, Peter felt sure that it was safe to take the pan off the stove. He poured the syrup through a sieve lined with two thicknesses of canton flannel and waited while the slow stream came through into the jar he had prepared to hold it.

Peter capped the jar and held it to the light. The syrup was so clear that he could see through it and the color was a shade darker than honey. The first sap ever made into syrup with his own hands! A pint boiled down from some twenty gallons of sap!

Wrapping the jar in a newspaper, he stowed it carefully in his rucksack; then he melted snow in the big pan on the stove and washed it and his other utensils. He shuttered the windows and left the sugar house in readiness for the next day; then he closed the door behind him. Outside, he put on his skis, hoisted the rucksack over his shoulders, and smiled as he felt the warmth of the jar of maple syrup against his back.

It was dusky in the woods as he made his way through them, and it seemed good to get into the open fields where daylight still lingered. The snow was hard and crusty, and his skis sang with speed as they cut their way. Never had he gone more exultantly than with the jar containing his first syrup on his back, yet never had he gone more carefully; for all his love of swiftness he would not risk a fall.

At one end of the field where he turned and crossed the brook to go through the pasture up to his father's farm, he suddenly decided not to turn but to go straight through the fields down to the valley. He wanted to take his first syrup to Mary and her grandmother. Perhaps they would ask him to stay and have supper with them. He smiled at the thought. It would be good to talk with people again. He had not uttered a word all day except in some brief one-sided conversation with a woods animal; and his ears had in them almost no other sound than the dripping of sap and its rumbling boil.

It was straight going now and a gentle incline as he followed the course of the brook through the open meadows. The snow cracked under his skis. Night was closing in about him. He felt that he was fleeing night in his race to warmth with something warm upon his back, something that he wanted to deliver while it was still warm. Reaching the familiar stone house, he took off his skis and stood them in a snowbank; then he knocked on the door.

Mary opened it. "Peter!" she exclaimed. "Come in."

As he was taking the rucksack from his back, Gran came from the kitchen, where she had been preparing supper. "I brought you something, Granny," Peter said.

"You have?"

He reached down into his rucksack for the jar, then he unwrapped it and held it out to her.

She took it from him and held it up to the light. "It's a fine color," she commented, "and the weight looks right too. But then you should be able to make good syrup. You've done it for years past with your mother, and no one around here has ever made any better syrup than she has."

"Oh, Granny, couldn't Peter stay and have supper with us?" Mary asked.

Peter grinned.

"Why, I expect he could." The tall gray-haired woman nodded slowly. "I've got a johnnycake in the oven and there's nothing goes better with it than maple syrup."

She went toward the kitchen with the jar in her hands. Before she reached the door, she turned and came back to Peter. "How much did you get today?"

"That pint," Peter replied, proud of his day's work.

"Then I'm not taking it, thank you," she said, handing it back to him.

"Why, Gran? I wanted it to be for you and Mary."

"It should go to your father. It's only right for the first fruits of the land to go to him who owns the land."

"But he—"

"You give that syrup to him," Gran said firmly. "It's his, no matter how much labor you put into it." She smiled.

"Bring us some next week. I can always make another johnnycake."

Peter went slowly on his skis up the hill to his home, taking them off and carrying them the last stretch. It was good to see the lights of the house streaming over the snow to meet him, and he was glad that there was still a little warmth in the jar on his back.

Things were humming in the kitchen. There was a pot of coffee on the stove and a frying pan with bacon sizzling in it. Andrew, with one of Martha's aprons tied around him and a cookbook open before him, stood by the table mixing something in a bowl.

"You're late," he said.

"It took longer than I thought it would," Peter replied, hoping he would not have to explain about the detour he had made to the village. He bent over to take the jar from the rucksack. "Here's the day's work," he said as he placed it on the table.

His father held it up to the light, turning it round and round, looking at it. "It seems all right," he murmured, "but we can't tell much until we taste it."

"What are you making?" Peter peered into the bowl.

"Pancake batter."

"Oh!" Then suddenly he said "Oh!" again. His father had known he would be bringing syrup home. He was making pancakes to go under it.

"Hungry?" Andrew asked.

"I'm as hungry as a horse," Peter answered.

3 Shep's Choice

The melting during the day and freezing at night put a fine hard crust on the snow. Peter went up to the maple grove on his snowshoes, carrying his skis over his shoulder. Everything was cold inside the sugar house, and it took him several minutes to get a good fire going in the stove. When it was roaring to his satisfaction, he stood before it, holding out his hands to the warmth. It was then that he thought he heard a small sound in the doorway. Turning quickly, he saw Shep. Her ears were laid back for she knew she had done wrong to follow him, but her tail was wagging in a plea for forgiveness.

"Oh, Shep," Peter said reproachfully.

She came toward him and he stroked her delightedly. She should not have come, but now that she was here, he was glad to have her company.

She had evidently slipped out of the door when he had left the house and had walked behind him on the hard crust, just far enough back so she would not be seen. Peter took her head in his hands and looked deep into her eyes. Did she really want to be with him, he wondered, or was she doing what so many animals do before they bring their young into the world—seeking for some hidden place in which to make their lair? If it were the latter, it would be hard to tell what might happen to the puppies with the nights so cold. Peter realized that he would have to watch her carefully lest, driven by her urge for secrecy, she retreat into the forest.

Shep sat down on the snow, her look one of dutiful obedience. Peter returned to his work. When he went out to start collecting the sap buckets, Shep followed him. Her keen ears had caught a sound in the pile of rocks where Peter had seen a blunt-nosed porcupine. Shep went across the snow to investigate.

"Shep, Shep," Peter called to no avail. Dropping everything, he ran across the snow and brought her back.

"I'm sorry, Shep, but you can't chase porcupines today," Peter admonished her, "and you shouldn't do it any day, for that matter."

Stretching her long heavy body out on the snow, Shep moved her tail in agreement and apology. Peter collected his buckets, emptying sap and ice into the big pan on the stove and returning the buckets to hang on the trees.

The slow day passed, as the one before it had, as presumably the rest of the days in the week would, and Peter, facing the challenge of quietness, found in it time and opportunity to observe the life of the forest. Had he been active or noisy, it would not have been apparent to him; but because he sat for long periods of time with Shep resting her head on his knee and only an occasional word spoken to her, his eyes and his ears could take in what was going on around him.

A crow flapped cawing above the treetops. Peter waved to it as one of the countryman's sure signs of spring. The pair of red squirrels came from their nests, raced down a maple's shaggy bark, and dived under the snow at its base. Peter thought they must have a network of tunnels under the snow, for their heads kept bobbing up in unexpected places; then with characteristic chuckles they would dart under the snow again, searching for remnants of food on the forest floor. The long-drawn, two-noted call that was the chickadee's spring song resounded often through the woods. Even the small black flies moving over the snow were evidences of the coming spring. A quickening was going on of much that had lain dormant. The world that had been silenced by winter was beginning to come alive again.

In the afternoon, when the sap had boiled down considerably, Peter made the round of the buckets, emptying their contents into the storage tank for the next day's boiling. If only he could stay up all night and keep the fire going under the evaporator, he told himself, what a lot he would have by morning. Then he heard Shep bark briefly and briskly, as if she were barking to herself. She had gone into the house and was standing by the stove, scratching at the earth floor.

Peter ran to her and knelt down beside her. She leaned against him and he ran his hand down her sides to comfort her. Under her silky coat her body was heaving convulsively. Startled, Peter looked anxiously about the sugar house. The puppies couldn't be coming like this—now, when he was alone—now, when the sap was boiling down to syrup!

"Shep, I've got to get you home quickly. Come on, Shep, come on."

Peter knew his fire would hold for some time, but he hoped that he could make the journey swiftly enough on his skis to be back before the sap thickened into syrup. He hoped, too, that he could manage to carry Shep through the woods. What, oh what, would his father say? But it was no use thinking of that now.

Shep did not follow him when he went to the door. Looking back at her, Peter knew with a sickening thud of realization that it was too late. If she had the puppies at all, she would have them in the sugar house.

"Oh, Mother, why aren't you here? Why did you have to go away?" Peter said aloud. His mother would have known what to do for Shep to make things easier for her.

Shep was panting. She looked up at Peter and her eyes implored him to stay near.

Peter reached up to a shelf where some burlap bags were lying. With them he made a nest in a corner of the sugar house where the floor was dry and there was warmth from the stove. Shep accepted it as hers. She turned round and round on the burlap, then scratched vigorously. After a moment she started to lick herself furiously, helping to draw into the world a small sac that held her first-born. She cut the sac quickly with her teeth, then she cut the cord with which the sac had been attached to her and through which the life within had been nourished. After swallowing the sac, she turned to licking her baby.

Faster and faster her long tongue moved around and underneath the limp object until it gave a little gasp, followed by a cry. Shep stopped her licking for a moment and wagged her tail. The little one was alive. It was breathing. Part of her work was done. She surveyed it proudly and drew her tongue gently over the small form. It was still wet and cold, but Shep would go on licking until it was dry and warm.

Shep looked up at Peter. She had not needed any help, but she was glad to know that someone she loved and trusted was standing near. Peter sighed with the swift wonder of it all: the way in which Shep had known exactly what to do. She was lying down now, tucking the puppy against her body, caressing it proudly with her tongue and cocking her ears at its small snuffling sounds.

Peter knelt down and ran his hand over her. "Good Shep," he said, "good dog."

Shep licked his hand. She needed no other comfort than those words.

With relief that Shep's first puppy was safely in the world, Peter turned back to the stove, where the thick foaming mass proclaimed itself to be at the syrup stage. He was glad that Shep did not require his near presence, for this was the time that the syrup demanded all his attention—stirring, testing, pouring, and then after the last drop had gone through the flannel, capping the jar.

By the time he had finished his work and could turn back to Shep, she had brought three other puppies into the world and was lying on her side with all four of them tucked against her body. At Peter's glance she wagged her tail slowly, happily, proudly, and nuzzled the puppies one by one so Peter could see how many there were. Then she pricked her ears and wagged her tail vigorously.

Peter heard the scraping sound of snowshoes. Running to the door, he looked out into the late afternoon light of the woods. The form of a man slightly bent but agile was coming toward the house.

"Benj!" Peter shouted joyously, for though he had not missed people during the long day, a rush of feeling swept over him when he realized that his lonely vigil was over.

Benj bent down to unbuckle his snowshoes. "Thought I'd come up to spell you a bit," he said. "Has it been a good day? How much have you made?"

"Come and see, Benj! Come and see!" Peter took hold of the mittened hand and drew Benj into the sugar house, so much darker than the woods that the old man squinted as he entered.

"A whole, big lovely quart of syrup," Peter said excitedly, "and Benj—four puppies!"

"Four puppies!"

Peter explained how Shep had followed him to the sugar house and though he had wanted to take her home, when she had begun acting queerly, there had not been time.

"Oh, Benj, I was awfully frightened. I didn't know what to do." It was a relief to Peter to be able to tell Benj how he felt and to know that Benj would not hold it against him.

Benj knelt down beside Shep and started fondling the puppies with Shep's full approval. "The little darlings," Benj murmured, crooning over them as he did with all young things. No matter how many the farm produced, or what kind—calf, colt, or lamb—there was always room in Benj's heart to welcome another brood or litter.

Holding the tiniest puppy up to his chin and letting his lips move over its silky domed head, Benj said, "You did all that anyone could do, Peter; you stood by and gave her confidence. That's strength and comfort enough for an animal. Whatever else they need they get from God."

"I—I felt so helpless."

"Well," Benj replied slowly, putting the puppy down and stroking Shep's head, "we've got to meet things alone as we go on through life. That's the way we discover that we're not alone."

Benj heaved off his rucksack and hung it on a peg, then bent over and picked up some wood. Just as he was opening the firebox of the stove to put it in, Peter placed his hand on his arm.

"Benj, I've finished my day's work. I'm ready to go home. There's no need to keep the fire up."

"Oh, yes, there is." Benj nodded knowingly. "I'm staying on and taking over where you leave off."

Peter's face widened with amazement and delight. "You mean you're going to keep boiling all night?"

"I do."

"Oh, Benj, that's good! There's sap in the storage tank and it's still flowing into the buckets. They'll be running over by morning if they're not emptied again."

Benj piled wood on the fire and shut the door of the box. The iron stove, which had been hot all day and had only begun to cool down, creaked and groaned as it took the heat again.

"Benj, you've been working all day. Aren't you tired? When will you sleep?"

An amused and throaty little laugh came from the old man. "When you get as old as I am, a little more or a little less sleep doesn't matter much. I'll sleep all right. Don't be concerned about me."

"There isn't any place to lie down," Peter said. His glance roved the sugar house, taking in the only things that offered a resting place on which to sit—the chopping block and the sawbuck with a slab of pine across it.

Benj's eyes twinkled as he looked at Peter. "I'm going to make myself a bough bed. But let's get some sap in the pan first so the heat won't go begging."

Together they made the round of the buckets. Benj slung the yoke over his shoulders and carried two buckets across the snow and into the sugar house. Peter carried a bucket in each hand. They worked quickly together and there was need, for twilight was already touching the woods, graying the snow and making the trees look tall and black. They poured as much sap into the pan as it would take, then they stood several full buckets beside the stove to be added as the sap boiled down.

Benj picked up the ax and ran his finger along the edge from force of habit. He went outside. Peter lit the kerosene lamp and looked over at Shep and her babies. Shep was standing up, panting again, and the babies were mewling around the burlap hunting for her.

Peter spread some more burlap quickly in an old wooden box and lifted the puppies into it. Shep did not seem to care what he did with them. Her sides heaved and she looked at Peter with troubled eyes.

"Benj! Oh, Benj!" Peter ran to the door and called into the darkness. "Shep's going to have another puppy."

Benj's ax could be heard, thudding against green bark. There was the sound and movement as a tree fell slowly and came to rest on the snow.

"Let her have it," Benj called back. "Come and give me a hand. Bring the hatchet with you."

Peter knelt down beside Shep and put his arms around her. "You'll be all right, girl, just the way you were before," he whispered. He picked up the hatchet and ran across the snow to join Benj.

"Are the four all right?"

"Yes, I put them in a box."

"Good."

Benj swung the ax and felled another small tree. Under Benj's directions, Peter topped and limbed the fallen trees until two sturdy logs some seven feet long and six inches in diameter lay along the snow; then they prepared two other logs of the same diameter but about five feet long. They cut a quantity of fir boughs and a small amount of spruce and hemlock. When Benj, surveying the lot, decided that they had enough, they dragged logs and boughs back to the sugar house.

The sap was boiling vigorously in the pan on the stove. The lantern was filling the house with warm light and deep shadows. Shep was licking her last puppy.

Benj cleared a corner in the house and laid the long logs parallel. Then he nailed the shorter logs to the ends of the long ones. The space between them he filled with the boughs they had limbed—fir, spruce, hemlock—pointing the butt ends toward the earth floor. The small boughs that had been cut at the last were laid on the top with their undersides up. The whole procedure took little more time than the making of a proper bed with sheets and blankets. When Peter saw how soft and springy and sweet smelling Benj's bough bed was, he longed to stay the night and share it; but there were a number of small reasons that made it necessary for him to get home as soon as possible.

Shep pushed her nose into his hand. He looked down at her quickly.

"Why, Shep," Peter said, "you shouldn't leave your baby all in the cold like that!"

Shep looked at him pleadingly, her tail wagging slowly. Then she turned around and went to the box where the four puppies were crawling, making snuffling sounds.

Peter looked over at the burlap in the corner. There the fifth puppy lay, stiff and unmoving.

"Oh, Benj," Peter said, "come quickly."

Benj left his work on the bed and knelt down beside the puppy. His hand was trembling as he reached out to pick it up. He held it to him for a moment, examining it closely. It seemed as perfect in its newborn way as the others, except that it did not share life with them.

"It never lived," Benj said quietly. He took an old handkerchief from his pocket and wrapped the small body in it.

"Can't you do anything for it?"

Benj shook his head. "Sometimes one can, but not when they're like this."

"Can't Shep?"

"She did all she could, all she knew how to do. When she saw it could not respond, she let it go. She isn't interested in it anymore. It's the others she wants to give herself to."

Benj laid the little shroud behind him. "I'll care for this later," he said. Reaching over he took the four puppies one by one from the box and laid them on the burlap. In a moment Shep stood over them, then shaping herself into a semicircle she lay down and gave them protection, thrusting them against her body with her long nose.

Peter still felt sick at heart and puzzled over the loss of the fifth puppy. It seemed cruel of Shep to turn away from it so casually and give herself to the others. It seemed odd of Benj to admit defeat when so often he had helped an animal to life.

Benj, still on his knees with the lamplight deepening the grooves in his face, looked up at Peter. "When we can do some good, Peter, the knowledge and the strength comes to us to work until we see the good accomplished; when we can't, the only thing for us to do is tend to our other jobs. Shep knows that. Look at her now! This little thing came into the world unable to respond to life. Shep realized that after a while and put it out of her mind."

"Couldn't Mother have made that puppy live—the way she did with my lamb Biddy? Remember how she worked with it when everyone thought it was dead?"

Benj shook his head. "Biddy was never lifeless. This little one was born dead. Sometimes, Peter, we can look what seems to be death in the face and challenge it. Sometimes we must look it in the face and say, 'So be it.' There's wisdom in both, and one learns after a time when to use the one wisdom and when the other."

Peter smiled at Benj. He felt better now about the puppy. He couldn't tell why, except that Benj made him see things clearly, even though he didn't always understand what he saw.

"You'd best be going," Benj reminded him. "Those puppies should be got back to the warm house where Shep can care for them better."

Peter nodded, knowing that even now his father might be wondering what had kept him so long. He buttoned his coat tight and drew on his mittens, while Benj packed the quart of syrup in the rucksack.

"Aye, you've got all kinds of produce for your father tonight," Benj said.

After Peter had buckled on his snowshoes, Benj handed him the puppies wrapped safely in several thicknesses of burlap. Peter tucked them inside his coat, thrusting in one hand to steady and control them. Shep whimpered a little at the procedure that resulted in the disappearance of her puppies, but Benj assured her that everything was all right. There was something about his tone that made her willing to accept his word, for she ceased whimpering. Then Peter started off, with Shep following him closely.

Before he reached the place where a turn in the path took the sugar house from view, he looked back for one last glimpse. There it stood, a dark rectangle against the darkness of the night with the white snow framing it. Benj was standing in the doorway. Behind him was the warmth and glow of the lantern and the clouds of steam that rose up from the pan on the stove. Peter waved with his free hand, but Benj did not see him in the darkness. Peter waved again, not to Benj now but to the sugar house itself, to the hours of work with their rich reward, to his skis standing expectantly in a snowbank. His wave was a salutation as well, a promise of early return.

He pictured Benj putting wood on the fire from time to time, adding to the sap in the pan from that in the buckets, snatching half- and quarter-hours of sleep on the bough bed, stirring, testing, and finally at some moment between the darkness of night and the paling of dawn arriving at the finished syrup. But he did not think of Benj as being alone. Somehow, no matter where he was, one never thought of Benj as being alone.

A puppy wriggled, and Peter stopped to make it secure. Shep, who had been following in Peter's snowshoe tracks, nuzzled against his legs for assurance that all was well with her family. Peter stroked the dog and spoke comfortingly to her, then he resumed his way, going slowly for Shep's sake. Once he had reached the open fields he could see lights from the house reaching across the snow like an outstretched hand. Cozy as it had been in the sugar house, the thought of home was welcoming. As Shep went up the slope, she stopped to rest more than once. Peter longed to carry her, but he could not with the four puppies inside his coat.

When he finally pushed open the door of the house, he called out to his father, but there was no answering sound. Peter felt almost glad that his father was out and that his arrival home would not be noticed. The kitchen bore the evidence of the meal Andrew had. One or two pots were still simmering on the stove and there were dishes in the sink.

Peter looked at the clock. It was after seven. Of course his father had supper and was now out in the barn making his nightly rounds. No wonder Peter felt hungry. He was glad that his father had left something on the stove for him.

Peter went to the box behind the stove and, kneeling beside it, took the puppies from inside his coat and laid them in the box. They started squirming around immediately, nosing and fumbling their way for the warm comforting bulk that was their mother. But Shep, tired as she was and eager to nestle down with her family, was hungry, and she stood waiting while Peter prepared her meal. She ate it greedily. Then, satisfied by the food and warmed by the glow of the stove, she crawled into the box and made the haven her puppies had been seeking.

Peter was washing his hands at the sink when his father came in from the barn, stamping his boots and shutting the door quickly behind him to keep the rush of sharp night air from entering the house with him.

"Hello, Father," Peter called to him, "come and see what I've brought home with me."

His father came into the kitchen. He looked tired and his face was lined. He saw the quart of syrup on the table. "That's better than you did yesterday," he said.

"Oh, but that isn't all! Look in Shep's box behind the stove."

His father walked over to the box. He looked in as if he could not believe what his eyes saw. "So that's what you've been up to!" he said to Shep. "I wondered where you had taken yourself." He reached down and stroked her behind her ears.

Peter dried his hands and came over to stand beside his father. "Aren't they nice puppies?"

"They are indeed. Where did you find her?"

"She followed me up to the sugar bush."

"Shep, Shep," his father said reproachfully, "what would Martha think if she knew you had your puppies up in the woods instead of in this warm house?"

"Perhaps she was lonely for Mother."

Andrew put his hand on Peter's head in a gesture he had not used since Peter had been a little boy. "Perhaps she thought you were lonely."

Peter dropped down to his knees and started fondling Shep. "I'm sorry you lost one of your babies."

"Did she have five?"

"Yes, Father, but Benj said the fifth one was born dead."

"Benj?"

"He came up to the sugar house after he finished work. He's staying there the night."

"I didn't want you to ask Benj for help," his father said, "I was going to try to get up myself tomorrow."

"I didn't ask him, Father. He just came."

"Benj is an old man. He shouldn't have a night of work after a long day."

"He made a bough bed. He's going to be comfortable."

"An old man needs a house and not a shack." His father looked worried. The lines across his brow deepened. There were times when his hope for the farm rested on Benj, the help he gave, the steadiness, the wisdom that had brought them through many difficulties. He could not afford to have anything happen to Benj.

Peter knew the look on his father's face. He saw the lines of worry drawn deep, but there seemed to be nothing he could do to ease those lines. He felt as helpless with his father as he had with Shep in travail.

"Shall I go back and tell Benj you don't want him to stay there all night?"

"No, no," his father said, "you've had a long enough day. Go to bed and get some sleep. You must be tired."

"I guess maybe I am." Peter gave Shep a last pat, then got to his feet and started up the stairs.

"Good night, Father."

"Good night, son."

Peter undressed slowly. He went to his window and, sitting down on the floor beside it, put his arms on the sill and gazed out. Beyond in the darkness was the woodland and Benj stoking the fire so the sap would boil, sleeping betweentimes on his bough bed, thinking the long sort of thoughts that made his face light up when he started to tell them. Peter's ears were still full of the rumbling of the sap. He felt sticky from the steam that had enveloped him. A delicious weariness came over him. His eyes closed.

There was a knock at the door. Peter moved his head slowly.

His father came into the room with a bowl in his hands. "You must be hungry," he said. "I brought you some supper."

Peter laughed sleepily and reached out his hand for the bowl. "I almost forgot."

His father put it in Peter's hands. "You've done a good day's work, Peter. I'm proud of you." Then he let one hand rest for a moment on Peter's head. He stroked the dark hair gently, and after a while he turned and left the room, going down the stairs on quiet feet.

Peter lifted the spoon to his mouth. It was meat stew his father had made for their supper and it was good!

4 The Best Ever

Early the next morning while his father was milking, Peter started on his chores—opening the drafts in the stove, getting a brisk fire going, bringing in wood from the shed. He let Shep out and, while she was gone, played with the puppies, who already seemed bigger and stronger. Andrew returned and Shep pushed past him, eager to join her babies. During breakfast, Peter told his father of his plans for the day.

"I'll do my best to get up and join you before the day is over," his father said.

"Is there anything I can do here to help you?" Peter asked, hoping in his heart that his father would say no.

Andrew shook his head. "You're doing one of the most needed tasks of the year and something that will please your mother."

"Perhaps there'll be a letter from her today."

His father smiled, not so much at Peter as at himself. "I'll be hoping for that every day, though she may not have time to write us more than once a week."

Peter left soon after breakfast. It was still early, but even then the sun was hot and the snow had begun to soften. He looked up into the blue sky above him with a wave of thankfulness that the day was good, that the sap would flow, and that before him lay whole hours wherein his sole work would be to draw out the hidden sweetness of the old maples and boil it down to syrup.

This was only the third morning he had gone sugaring, but, Peter thought to himself as he went over the snow, how different each morning had been. The snow had not always the same whiteness nor the sky the same blueness; the shifting shapes of the clouds were varied; even the wind in the treetops had an unusual sound. Drawing near the woods he heard a commotion in one of the trees. It sounded like nothing so much as a hundred squeaky doors opening and closing. Looking up, he saw that the bare limbs were covered with grackles, not in dozens but in scores. A migrating flock had stopped to rest.

"Welcome to our countryside," Peter called up to them, greeting them cheerfully. Harsh of voice as they were and far from beautiful, they bore the promise of spring that all nature seemed to be speaking.

The grackles went on with their chatter, oblivious to the boy standing in the snow beneath them.

Before entering the woods, Peter stood still and looked around him. It was so much warmer this morning than the other mornings. The sap would flow faster today. Peter thought back to the very first morning when he had skied up to the sugar bush before sunrise. Alone on the brink of a great adventure, he had met the coldest moment of the day and exulted in it. The dawn wind, searching and bitter, had swept around him, piercing mittens, wool cap, and sturdy parka. Springing from the east, the wind had swept down the valley like a stiff broom, seeking the relics of night and dispersing them.

This morning the sun was already up, and it was challenging Peter to keep pace with it. Each successive morning it would rise a fraction farther north, giving more light to the world and more hours to the day.

Peter started into the woods, feeling then as if no day could be long enough for him with all he wanted to do.

By the time he reached the sugar house he was out of breath and warm from the speed he had made. Flinging open his coat, he called a good morning to Benj.

Benj pointed with pride to the jars of syrup he had capped. "We'll have something to show your mother when she gets back," he said, his eyes twinkling, "even if we are only doing the sugaring in a small way this year."

"Benj, that's grand!" Peter exclaimed.

Peter wanted to know how Benj had slept on the bough bed, and Benj wanted to know how the puppies had fared.

"Did you really sleep much?" Peter queried.

"Off and on."

"What did you do all the rest of the time?"

"When it was dark I watched the stars. For the past hour or two I've been watching the light come through the woods."

Benj made no other comment. There was something in his face that said he had partaken of wonder as another might partake of food. To see night dissolved by dawn, to see dawn melt into day, left its mark on a man.

"I've had plenty to do one way or another," Benj said, "not to mention the boiling."

"It's odd how much can happen up here," Peter said.

Benj told Peter he had watched a woodchuck make a trial excursion from his burrow. "But he went back again quickly enough. I guess he feels the world has a lot of warming to do before it will suit him." He showed Peter where deer had browsed on twigs and the foliage of evergreens. "Just when the light was breaking they came, so gentle and easy. I would have stroked them if I could, but they wouldn't understand."

"Oh, yes they would, Benj! I think any animal would understand you."

"Not the wild ones, Peter." He shook his head. "They live in their own way, and it's a different way from ours. But we can watch them and take a lot to ourselves about their ways."

Peter told him of the grackles he had seen.

"Did you, now? And I saw a flock of geese heading north. Oh, yes indeed, the world has made its turn and we're getting into spring. There'll be only another few days of sugaring with the way things are going now. Soon the trees will be wanting all the sap for their leaves."

They could have talked through the morning, but each knew the other had work to do—Benj, his farm chores, Peter, his boiling. While Benj got ready to leave, Peter made the round of the buckets on the trees and brought what sap had collected in them back to the house; then he stoked the fire. Standing in the doorway, he watched Benj trudge off over the softening snow as Benj had watched him the night before.

Peter's hands hung limp at his sides, and he felt that a day lay before him with little to do. Suddenly he was aware of a sharp sense of loneliness. For the first time since he had been at the sugar house he felt alone. Yesterday there had been Shep; the day before that there had been the thrill and the newness to keep him company. Today there was the realization that he was by himself and that it would be many hours before Benj would return.

Peter waved to Benj and the old man waved back.

Watching Benj go through the woods, Peter began to wonder what life would be like without Benj. He had never thought of that before. He had accepted Benj as he had everything else in his life. Benj belonged; he had always been part of the farm, he always would be. But the fact of his mother's being away brought hard knowledge to Peter of the impermanence of even those things thought to be permanent. Someday Benj might not be with them.

"Benj!" Peter shouted through the woods, holding on to the retreating figure with a shred of sound.

Benj turned and waved. "A good day to you, Peter. I'll be back by evening."

Peter felt comforted. Benj would return. Benj always kept his word. With a lighter heart he turned to his work of gathering wood and having it in readiness to feed to the fire.

The sap flowed from the trees that day, not in drops but in tiny streams, and by noon the buckets were full. Peter stored some and added the rest to the sap in the boiling pan. He was glad that the fire would be continued through the night so the sap would all be used.

Late in the day, just as the sugar stage was approaching, he heard voices through the woods, shouts and laughter. Mary appeared with Randy and the twins, Sam and Sue.

"Hello, Peter!" they shouted.

Peter could hardly believe his eyes when he saw them. He called out to them excitedly and waved both hands in the air for a welcome. Then, remembering that he could not leave the stove for long, he darted back into the sugar house to stand by the boiling pan. "This has got to be the best syrup ever," he said to himself, as he stirred and tested.

The boys and girls unbuckled their snowshoes and stood them in a snowbank. Peter joined them with some of the hot syrup in a small tin pan. Finding a clean untrodden piece of snow, he poured the syrup on it. All five watched and waited as it hardened slowly.

"Help yourselves," Peter said.

They reached over and twisted off sections, eating it like candy. Smiling with pleasure at the taste of it, all of them turned to Randy and waited for him to pass judgment.

The tall boy savored it keenly, then he leaned over and broke off another section. He had a thoughtful look on his face as he measured the maple flavor against the memory of other maple flavors. Satisfied at last, he turned to Peter.

"If I do say it myself, I've never tasted any better."

"You mean it's as good as the syrup you've been making this year?"

"Every bit," Randy replied stoutly, "if not better."

Peter sighed. He had not realized how much he had been counting on Randy's approval.

"But it isn't entirely your doing, Peter," Randy reminded him. "Everyone has always said your father's maples are the sweetest in this countryside."

"Do you think I've got the weight right?"

"Seems so," Randy said, "but it's hard to tell when you're so stingy with it."

Delighted at Randy's approval, Peter went back to the stove. He filled two small pans full of syrup and brought them out to pour on the snow.

"Have some more, have all you can eat," he urged generously. "There's plenty of sap in the trees and plenty of wood for the fire."

Sam had found two smooth sticks, paddles he called them. Dipping one into the syrup, he used the other to help fold the rapidly hardening syrup around the first stick. "This is the best way to eat it," he announced.

The others were soon following his example, wrapping a stick with the maple candy and sucking it. Peter brought out more syrup.

"Oh!" Mary exclaimed suddenly. "I almost forgot what Granny gave me." She reached into her pocket and produced a small jar of pickles.

"Whatever are they for?" Sue asked.

"Good enough!" Randy shouted. "Your grandmother knows what's needed in a sugar bush."

"But pickles! Now?" Sue was still puzzled.

"If something sour you eat, you'll have more room for sweet," Randy chanted.

They ate some of the pickles, and then Peter brought out more syrup to be paddled or cooled on the snow. The sharp taste of the pickles whetted their appetites for the sugar.

After his friends had left, Peter looked at the pan on the stove. The level had gone down alarmingly, but even so there was still enough for him to bottle a quart before Benj came. What a lot he would have to tell Benj, he thought, and his father if he came would be interested to know of Sam's method of paddling.

The hope that his father would accompany Benj gave him an extra eagerness during the remaining hour, but as twilight came down through the woods only Benj appeared.

"Your father said to tell you he was sorry, Peter, that he couldn't get up," Benj said, then he chuckled, "but he'll be here one of these nights. He'll not be able to keep away any more than I could. This old sugar house calls to one this time of the year."

"Did he mind your coming?"

"Mind?" Benj laughed. "He knows I've got to come." Benj saw the quart of syrup. "That's the best color yet. I'll have one to match it by morning."

When Peter got back to the farmhouse that evening, he found a letter from his mother. He looked at it lying on the table in the kitchen, bearing his own name in the careful writing that he knew well but had not often seen directed to him. He sat down on the floor beside the puppy box, fondling Shep while he turned the pages and read his mother's message.

She was glad he was looking after the sugaring; that was one big load off her mind. She hoped the puppies had come and that they were doing well. She did not know when she would be able to leave. Uncle Leonard was far from well. Several ribs had been broken in the accident, and though they were mending slowly, pneumonia had set in and he required constant care. It did not look as if he would gain rapidly enough to let her be home for the spring chores. But she would be home in time to get the garden in, of that she was sure, and she had told Andrew about the seeds. Her thoughts were with them most of the time, and she hoped they were getting on all right and that Peter was helping his father.

He read her next words slowly.

Remember, Peter, to help your father where you can. When you can't see what to do, wait for him to tell you. He's got confidence in you, but it may not always show. It's like syrup. It's there all right, in all that sap, but it takes a deal of boiling to bring it out; and it takes a good fire to keep the boiling going. I suppose that, with people, understanding is like the fire in the stove: it keeps things alive until the essence can be drawn out.

Peter read that part of his mother's letter over and over. That was like her, he thought, to be so sure that the sweetness was there—in a maple tree or a man—and to keep on doing what she could until it got down to that. What did she call it? He looked again at her letter. "The essence." Peter smiled. Benj would like that. He would have to show him the letter tomorrow.

Peter took the puppies out of their pen and let them crawl over him. Shep stood by and nosed them back toward Peter when they started to roam. His father came in and stood watching them.

"Did you find your mother's letter?"

"Yes, Father."

"I had one from her too. She says she won't be able to come home for a while."

"Maybe not until it's time to get the garden in."

"That's too far away," his father said. He turned to start preparations for their evening meal.

"Shall I lay the table, Father?"

"I'd be glad if you would, Peter."

Peter put the puppies back in their box and stroked Shep, then he washed his hands and started to set dishes and cutlery on the table, trying to remember what his mother had said about helping in the way his father might want him to help.

They sat for a long time over their supper that night, talking about one thing and another; then Peter did the dishes while Andrew went out to the barn on the nightly round. When he returned, they drew their chairs up again to the kitchen table and opened a checkerboard between them, beginning the first of a series of games. And though the next hour was spent mostly in silence, it was a silence of understanding and companionship. Martha's letters had brought something of her presence into the household, and the kitchen was a friendlier place than it had been since she went away.

Day after day during the week of school vacation Peter worked in the sugar bush; night after night Benj came up to continue the work. On the last day, Peter worked harder than ever and Benj came up earlier.

"Your father is joining us in a little while," Benj announced when he arrived. "I told him we'd cook him some supper on the stove if we got our boiling done in time."

Peter looked pleased. "What can we give him, Benj?"

"Just what we'd give ourselves and what I brought along in my sack."

Peter watched him unpack and saw what he had brought for their meal. There was a jar of pancake batter, some strips of bacon, coffee for the pot, and a bottle of milk.

"I didn't bring any syrup for the cakes," Benj said. "I knew we'd have our own."

It was dusk when Andrew arrived at the sugar house. The snow had gone down so far during the week that he wore neither skis nor snowshoes, just stout boots that laced nearly up to his knees. He stood in the doorway watching Peter and Benj as they capped the four quarts into which their day's run had been poured. In a smaller jar Benj had put what syrup remained for them to use that evening.

"Am I too late?" Andrew asked.

"Never too late," Benj answered. "I'm going to get our supper ready now, and while I do that you and Peter might go around and get the spigots from the trees and collect the buckets. We'll fill the big pan with snow and get enough boiling water to wash everything out and leave things ready for next year."

Peter smiled as he heard Benj giving orders. Generally it was the reverse—Benj did what Andrew told him to do. But the sugar house was Benj's province at present, and he it was who issued instructions on what would be done there.

Benj prepared the meal while Peter and his father trudged off silently into the woods. They took the buckets from the trees, emptying the sap onto the snow. They drew out the spigots and put them all into a basket. Working in relays, they got their equipment back to the sugar house. There was just enough light left to guide them in their work, but it was fading fast and the day was going down to cold and dampness.

When they returned to the house from their last trip, it was a welcome thing to stand by the stove and watch pancakes being made. Benj poured the batter on the griddle with a careful hand, then with zest in his eyes he watched until the pancakes were ready to be turned. He had a tin plate piled high with golden, crisp-edged cakes at the back of the stove, and there was still a little batter left in the jar.

Peter could not remember when pancakes and bacon and maple syrup had ever tasted so good, but whether it was because he was hungry or because of the warmth in the sugar house or because of the conversation between Benj and his father he could not tell. A kind of peace had settled over them all, a peace of accomplishment. The work must end though the sap was still flowing, but neither Peter nor Benj felt any regret. They had done the best they could in the time they had allotted to themselves and that, as Benj had said, was all that any man could do. Standing in a row, ready to be taken home, were quart jars totaling four gallons of maple syrup. That was just four gallons more than nothing, Peter told himself, and including what he'd already taken home, it was enough to take them through to the next sap season.

Sometimes he listened to his father and Benj in their talk; sometimes he dreamed as his eyes gazed into the shadowy distances; sometimes he just poured more syrup on a stack of pancakes and ate as if he would never have enough.

"Well, Benj," his father was saying, "we'll be breeding Buttercup Princess before too long."

"I didn't think there was a bull within ten miles good enough to serve her," Benj said proudly. "Have you discovered one?"

"Yes, I have," Andrew replied, "over at Green Mead Farm. He's won every blue ribbon the county can offer and not a few in the state, and his progeny are already making records. Whether he sires a bull or a heifer, it will bring a fine strain into our herd."

"But Green Mead is twenty-five miles distant if it's a mile!" Benj exclaimed. "That's a long way to take a cow to be bred."

Andrew nodded. "It's that far if you go by the road around the mountain, but, Benj, there used to be a path along the brook at the back side of the mountain. If we could lead her over that, it wouldn't be more than a few miles."

"Maybe not, but that path hasn't been used in years."

"A few days of work on it and we could open it up again."

Benj shook his head. "That path was once thought to be dangerous."

"What do you mean?"

"Rattlers used to live on that side of the mountain and they're not good for man or beast."

Andrew threw back his head and laughed loud and heartily. "The rattlers were cleaned out years ago, Benj. My own father told me so."

Benj said nothing but his head shook slowly, rhythmically, as if it were the pendulum of a clock.

Peter leaned closer to his father. "Maybe we could open up the path," he said hopefully.

"Maybe we could, Peter. We'll have a look at it one of these days." Andrew gazed at his son proudly. He had not thought Peter could do the sugaring, but more than four gallons of syrup were their own proof.

"There's trouble enough," Benj said, "without going out of your way to find more."

"Peter and I may prove to be a match for any trouble."

Peter felt as if his heart would swell his jacket out when he heard his father's words.

"Is there no bull nearer than Green Mead?" Benj asked.

"No bull I want for Buttercup Princess."

Benj smiled and put his hand on Andrew's shoulder. "So be it then," he said, "and you'll have the strength of my arms to help you do whatever you want to do."

"Mine too," Peter added.

They finished their supper, then washed the buckets and spigots, the ladles, the thermometer, and everything that had been used in the sugaring. The big boiling pan was turned upside down to dry out in the warmth of the sugar house. They packed the jars of syrup in a box which Peter and Andrew would carry between them. They put out the lamp and saw that the fire had gone to embers in the stove, then, heaving on their rucksacks, they made their way through the woods. Benj went first. He had an uncanny knowledge of the country and even in darkness could not lose his way. Each one of them walked carefully; Benj as he led, Peter and Andrew as they carried between them one of the farm's most precious crops.

Peter's heart was singing as he walked. They were going to clear a path in the woods over which Buttercup Princess might be led to Green Mead Farm. Her calf, when it came, would be the beginning of a strong strain in their herd. Peter was to have a part in bringing this about as he helped his father open the old path. This was what his mother had said might be a turning point in his father's life. So much had failed or been hard going, but if the herd could thrive, that would bring new life to the farm.

5 Peter's Plan

April came with welcome warmth and frequent showers that turned the world from white to green, making leafless twigs to swell with the promise that summer would fulfill. Shep could have her puppies outside with her, and Peter built a pen for them with walls high enough to keep the babies in but low enough to let their mother get to them. Shep was not feeding them now, for the puppies were grown enough to feed themselves, and four times a day all of them ate noisily around a single plate; yet Shep still liked to spend most of her time with them. She would wash them tirelessly in the hope that some day they would learn to care for themselves; then she would lie on her side in the pen and let them crawl all over her. Playing their own version of hide-and-seek, the puppies would cry pitifully at a bewildering separation of a few inches from each other amid the confusion of their mother's long coat; then, discovering one another again, they would squeal with delight and tumble together in a heap.

In the woods the delicate white and pink flowers of the hepatica could be found, sometimes under snow that had not yet retreated. At night the barking of foxes seeking their mates made a curious symphony of sound with the peepers who were busily accounting for the long months of quiet with hours of ceaseless conversation. Birds came searching for summer homes. Swallows were looking over the old nests high in the rafters of the barn; in the orchard flashes of blue, more brilliant than the sky, proclaimed the arrival of the bluebirds. Along the brook pussy willows were in bloom, and the twisted horns of the skunk cabbage were uncurling. By the time May came to the mountain world, nature was lavish with warmth and foliage and Benj was ready to plant the garden.

"But surely Mother will be home for the planting," Peter said one Friday afternoon to his father.

They were sitting at the kitchen table assembling seeds. Before them in packets lay the new ones that had been ordered during the winter; others that had been saved from the previous year were in a series of small glass jars carefully labeled in Martha's handwriting.

His father shook his head. "Once we thought we couldn't spare her. Now that's what they think."

"But if Uncle Leonard is so much better, why can't she come home?"

"The pneumonia left him in such a weakened condition that they want your mother to stay until he is strong again." His father nodded as if in approval of their decision. "There was a time when no one but Martha thought he would recover. Now that she has him mending they want to keep her there." He smiled. "Besides, there'll soon be a new baby for her to look after."

"Well," Peter said philosophically, "if she has that, she won't mind so much having missed Shep's puppies when they were tiny."

Peter felt proud of what his mother could do to make people well. He remembered the lamb that she had nursed into liveliness and that had been his pet and then the leader of the flock for so many years. He had seen her care for other animals who were ailing, and he knew what her skilled fingers could do with plants that had drooped. He remembered how her hands felt when he had been fevered. Benj said it was because she stood so close to God. Whatever it might be, Peter knew that where his mother was, there was comfort that went deeper than any words. He missed her fully as much as his father did; yet there was a pleased feeling within him, as there was with Andrew, that another household should be knowing what they had known for years.

"She'll be sorry not to be here when we plant the garden, won't she?" Peter asked.

"She will indeed," Andrew replied, "but she'll not let the earth be idle, nor her own hands. She'll make a garden where she is." Andrew placed the last packet of seeds in the basket, "There now, everything's there from carrots to corn, and if the day is fair tomorrow, you and Benj should have the garden in by night. And I think it will be fair."

"Aren't you going to help us?"

"No." His father shook his head. "I've got other work to do."

"Oh, Father!" Peter exclaimed, disappointed that his father would not be with them when the seeds went into the ground.

"Benj will help you."

"Yes, I know. He'll do most of it; he always does."

"Save him where you can, Peter. Benj is too old to do much hard work."

"I will, Father."

Peter went out to the hens, whistling as he crossed the space between the house and the barn. He shouldn't mind, he told himself, that his father was busy on the day the garden was to be planted. It was just that there was something wondrous about the putting of seeds in the soil. He remembered how his mother had gone about it—on her knees, with her hands resting lightly on the earth as she placed the seeds in the rows Benj had prepared, and a look on her face that was like the look she had in church on Sunday. It was as if something down inside her was happy.

As Peter thought about it, he recalled that there were many times when his mother's face bore that same expression. He had seen it when she was planting the garden, or standing over a kettle of boiling jam, or when she was caring for something that had been hurt. It was a look of peace, a look of thankfulness. Peter began to think of his mother as one who had Sunday always in her heart.

"Hello, Blondie!"

At the sound of his voice the hens looked up from their scratching in the earth. One by one they came toward him, Copper Queen and Amazon, Squawker, and all the dozen that composed the laying flock. They bent their heads and gazed at him, flicking their eyes, making cooing sounds. Peter reached out his hand to stroke their rich, glossy feathers. They squatted, one by one, under the touch of the friendly hands, then they made throaty sounds of contentment.

Peter was proud of the hens. Their molt was over and they were all in full feather. Their plumage glistened in the strong light of the setting sun; their combs and wattles were a bright red, their legs a healthy yellow. And they were giving eggs now, ten and more a day. Peter and his father used what they needed and the surplus was stored in a crock in the cellar against the day when the hens would not supply their need.

With dignity the hens walked away from Peter and re-sumed their activities, scratching in the earth for slugs or worms, digging hollows to settle into for a dust bath. Blondie stood looking at Peter, her golden plumage shining.

Peter reached into his pocket and tossed some bits of bread toward his favorite hen. "I didn't forget you, Blondie, but don't tell the others."

The next morning was fair, as Andrew had thought it would be. The sun was warm. No clouds ventured across the sky, and only the lightest of breezes ruffled the new leaves on the trees. Peter and Benj went to the plot of ground at one side of the house that had for many years been the vegetable garden. Between them they carried their tools and the basket of seeds.

In the fall of the year when the crops were harvested, the ground was raked thoroughly, then seeded to winter rye; over it all was spread a rich dark blanket of manure. In the early spring, after the frost and dampness had gone out of the ground, Benj would plow under the thick green growth of winter rye that had pushed up through the manure; then he would harrow it until the earth was soft and friable. There it would rest under the ministry of the sun until the time for planting came.

Benj stood at the edge of the garden, moving one foot around in the earth. "It's ready enough," he said, proud of the soil and of the work that had put it into condition. "It's fairly asking for the seeds." He looked up at the sun, high and powerful in the wide expanse of sky above them. "And the sun is up there waiting to help them grow."

Peter knelt down and cupped a handful of soil in his fingers, then he separated his fingers and let it run out between them. "It feels ready," he said. He, too, felt a thrill of pride, for this was earth that was his father's, and in a certain way that made it his.

They measured out their rows, marking them with a line and making depressions where the seeds were to go. When seeds were to be planted in hills, such as corn and squash and melons, they measured the distances between the hills. Once the work of planting began, Benj did much of it on his knees. Peter found it easier to bend over and drop the seeds in the rows, but Benj moved along a row at his own pace and in his own fashion.

Peter teased him about it, saying it was slow and clumsy.

Benj chuckled, leaning back on his heels to take a moment's rest. "Knees are something a gardener comes to sooner or later, Peter," he said, as he spread a covering of earth over some squash seeds he had just put in, smoothing the earth down with his hands. "Good humus—that's the soil—and humility—that's something you feel when you're on your knees—go together like a team in harness."

Peter watched him and listened.

Benj reached into a pocket for another handful of seeds and moved on to the next hill. "Did you ever think, Peter, that a seed can't start reaching up to the sun until something in it has gone down first into the earth?" Benj nodded his head. "I'm not sure that a man can go far if he hasn't first learned to bow before something bigger than he is."

Peter's eyes twinkled. "No wonder you and Mother used to take so long to plant the garden if you stopped and talked like this!"

Benj nodded. "Martha said to me once that she thought our garden did well because of all we gave the seeds to think about when they were in the earth."

Peter laughed and turned back to his work.

Sighing happily, Benj put his handful of seeds in the ground and moved on down the row. Pleased with the feel of the seeds, he was not so aware of them as he was of the plants they would grow to be, good to look upon in their midsummer strength and good to eat when they reached the table under Martha's knowing hands.

When Peter finished his work he took off his shoes and walked around the edge of the garden, letting the sun-warmed soil squeeze up between his toes, watching the impress of his feet on the earth and idly drawing pictures with his toes. Benj met him at the end of a row. His lined old face was beaded with sweat and the knees of his dungarees were the same color as the soil.

Together they surveyed their work. The seeds were all in and neatly covered, the rows tamped down by the flat of a hoe and the hills hand-smoothed. They knew that all they could do was done. Now they would wait for the sun and soil and rain to work the changes, bringing carrots and beets, onions and cabbages out of the same earth and in the same manner, yet making them distinct in color, shape, and taste. Ahead of them was the time for cultivating and weeding, for thinning and transplanting; far, far ahead of them was the time for harvesting. At present it was enough to know that the seeds had been entrusted to the soil.

They parted; Peter went to do his usual afternoon chores of sweeping the barn floor and filling the wood box in the kitchen. When they were done, he would go to the hens and entice them into their pen with a handful of grain. Benj took the rake and spade and went to the flower beds near the house to ready them for planting. Flowers would bloom in the dooryard whether Martha was there to see them or not, Benj was determined. And he had time to care for them. The week before, the sheep had gone up to the high pasture and, except for an occasional visit to them, they would take care of themselves through most of the summer. Benj had locked the door of his own little house and come to stay at the farm so he could help Andrew more and do many of the tasks that would have been Martha's had she been there.

That night at supper Peter told his father about the garden. His father was pleased.

"Your mother will be glad to know that."

"I'm going to write her a letter and tell her all about it."

"Tell her for me—" his father began, then he stopped short. No need to trouble Peter with his worries. No need to tell Martha about them either, except that they had a way of lessening when he voiced them to her.

Peter saw the line deepen across his father's brow. "What shall I tell her?"

He shook his head. "I'll be writing her myself tomorrow."

Peter started to clear the table.

"How are the hens?" his father asked suddenly.

"Laying well," Peter replied.

"None of them off their feed?"

"No."

"That's good."

"Why, Father?"

"In the village today I learned of a disease that's been playing havoc with some of the flocks in this countryside."

Peter felt a cold fearfulness within him.

"Nothing to worry about," his father went on. "Just let me know if any of them look poorly."

"If anyone does, should I separate her from the others?"

"By all means, and let me know immediately. I'll have Benj take care of her."

Peter bit his lip hard. That meant only one thing: the chopping block, a hastily dug trench, a bag of lime, and the muted, thudding sound as a spade turned the fresh earth back into the trench. "Not Blondie," he found himself saying inwardly; then all their names rushed through his mind. "Not any of them, please."

His father soon retired behind the widespread pages of his farm paper, and Peter sat on the floor to play with Shep and the puppies.

"Father," Peter said, after there had been silence between them for a while. "Now that the garden's in and school will soon be over, can't we start working on that path along the brook?"

"What path?" Andrew asked, his thoughts more on the printed words before him than on the question voiced by his son.

"The path between our farm and Green Mead."

His father put the paper down. "Yes," he said slowly as he recalled their earlier conversation about it. "Yes. We need that path if we're ever to have a link between the two farms."

"Couldn't we start tomorrow, Father?"

"Tomorrow's Sunday."

"Well then, Monday after school?"

"Benj and I are going up to dip the sheep Monday. We won't be home until dark."

Peter was silent. Tuesday seemed too distant even to mention.

His father put a hand across his head. "I don't know, Peter, when I'll have time to help you with it. The days aren't long enough for all the things I have to do. There just aren't the hours for the things I'd like to do."

"Maybe—maybe—" Peter spoke slowly, for the idea that had come to him was so startling that he could scarcely voice it. "Maybe I could open up that path myself."

Andrew looked at him intently, almost as if he were measuring the small boy he had known Peter to be against the man he was becoming. "You did the sugaring almost single-handedly."

Peter smiled. He could feel the warm glow of pleasure from his father's words moving through him. It made his face feel as if he were sitting before a blazing fire.

"The sugaring was fun," he said lightly.

"I wish you could make a start on the path, Peter. I'll be able to help you with some of it later on, I'm sure. And Benj is a good hand at brush burning."

Peter clenched the fingers of his right hand as if they were closing around an ax handle.

"Father, is there anything in what Benj says about rattlers on that side of the mountain?"

His father shook his head. The tired lines of his face eased themselves into a smile. "Not a thing," he said. "There were rattlers there years ago, but my father had them all cleaned out. He wouldn't have such on his land. No more would I."

"But why does Benj—"

"Benj is an old man," Andrew interrupted, "and his eyes are not so good as they once were, or his hearing, for that matter. He probably saw a black snake and thought it was a rattler."

"Are there black snakes over there?"

"Most likely, but they're harmless. They'll do no more than give you a start when you see them sliding over the ground."

Peter shivered. "I'd like to try opening that path for you."

"Would you?"

Peter nodded. "It would be fun."

"Don't do it at the cost of your other farm work."

"No, I'll do it just in my spare time," Peter promised. That would be the time he might spend with his friends, he realized, but he felt then that he wouldn't mind if he didn't see much of them during the summer if he could do something to help his father.

"Have a care while you work," his father said, picking up his paper again.

"I shall."

After a few moments, Peter murmured good night and started up the stairs to bed.

"Sleep well," his father called after him.

In the cool darkness of his room, Peter began thinking of the path along the brook. His father had said that night at the sugar house that the distance to Green Mead was short enough to lead a cow there and back in a day. If he, Peter, could find traces of the old road that once ran between the farms it should not take him more than his free time during the summer to clear it. Too excited to sleep, he looked out of the window at the mountains, a high curved line against the sky, and made his pact with them.

He wished he could talk about his plan with his mother. She would be eager about it and as interested in it as he was. Thinking of his mother made him conscious of how much he missed her. He put his hands to his eyes. They were hot and burning. He wanted her to be near. He wanted to talk with her, hear her voice. He didn't want to miss her like this, but he did—he did. Suddenly he put his head down. He was too old to cry. No, not too old to cry, he told himself; but too old to have anyone see him crying.

After a while, when the ache within him had eased, he decided to go downstairs and see what kind of an edge his ax had on it. Peter went down the stairs quietly, though he knew that nothing would disturb his father when he was engrossed in his farm paper. He groped his way through the dark woodshed until he came to the chopping block with a heavy ax sunk deep and safe into the center of the wood. He did not try to release it for this was his father's ax. Beside it was a lighter one. Peter pulled it from the wood and ran his fingers around the edge of the blade. It was keen, though it could stand to be even sharper for the work that was before it. Satisfied, he went back to his room and got into bed.

Almost before he knew he had gone to sleep, the sun came over the mountains, looking in at the window and telling him that a new day had begun.

6 Facing the Challenge

Days of rain and days of the sun's long shining brought the garden along well. Where the seeds had been planted so carefully there appeared a breaking of the soil, then a few spears of green, followed by the unfolding of the first set of leaves, and after that the characteristic structure of the plants. Only an inch above the ground, a carrot proclaimed itself as such, and the other vegetables were equally distinctive. Benj walked up and down between the rows in the morning and in the evening, often dropping to his knees to observe more closely what was going on. He would smile to himself at what he saw, as happy over the promise in the garden as he was over the baby chicks that were hatching in the hen house.

All through the month of May and far into June the weather was perfect, so much so that Andrew began to shake his head and say it couldn't last.

Benj shook his head too, but in disagreement. "These fine days can't be taken from us," he said, "no matter what happens later."

The type of the day mattered little to Peter. Each one brought him nearer the final one that marked the end of the school year.

Along the brook, ferns had uncurled and were waving their delicate plumes in the cool air that moved near the water.

Cress grew green and fresh in the brook, and Peter went down often in the late afternoon to collect a handful for their evening meal. The cows gave rich milk these days, for the grass in the pastures was lush. It was a good time on the farm.

On the morning of that last day of school, the household was a busy place. Andrew and Benj were driving over in the truck to Green Mead, taking two of Shep's puppies with them. A third puppy was being given to Mary and her grandmother.

Shep had made her own choice of the four. From the time they had begun to crawl, there was one she had always seemed to enjoy more than the others. Not that she singled it out for extra care, but for longer games. As they grew, the youngster— whom Peter had named Dusty because of the gray tinge to his coat—had been more attentive to Shep while the others played together. So, when it came time for the pups to go to new homes, Dusty was the one who remained with Shep.

Shep and Dusty sat on the doorstep together and watched unconcernedly as Andrew loaded the box with the two puppies in it into the truck, and Peter climbed in with the third pup on his lap. Benj came from the garden with a basket containing the first radishes, some spinach, and a few small lettuces. They were fresh, green, and shining with the dew still on them, and he wanted Mary and Gran to share the garden's first yield.

They were driving down the road to the village when Peter remembered to tell his father that one of the hens, Squawker, had shown no interest in her food that morning.

"Perhaps she had a full crop," Andrew said.

When they reached the stone house in the village, it was hard to tell which caused more excitement—the puppy with Mary or the basket of vegetables with her grandmother; but school was still in session, whether it was the last day or not, and soon Mary and Peter, waving good-by, raced off to the schoolhouse. The puppy barked excitedly and wanted to follow them, but Gran held it tightly in her arms.

Mary looked back longingly.

"The puppy will be here when you get back," Gran said.

"Don't wait supper for us, Peter," his father called after him. "We may not be back until late."

"I'll see that he has a good stout meal this noon," Gran said, "then he won't be needing too much later on."

Andrew laughed. He could remember having one of Gran's meals when he'd been a boy. There were no empty places within him to be filled then. He had felt firm and tight all over and ready for a job of work.

"There's time for you and Benj to have a cup of coffee and a piece of my cinnamon cake," Gran said, "and to give me the news of Martha."

Andrew thought, as he sat at the table, that at Gran's house there always seemed to be time for such things. "I don't expect Martha back now until the end of the summer," he said. "She's got her hands full there and she's doing a fine piece of work."

"You and Benj must have your hands full, too, to get your work done as well as hers."

"Peter has been more of a help than I ever thought he could be."

"That's the way with the young ones," Gran said. "Let them know you rely on them and they'll show you how much they can do."

"Sometimes I think it was almost a good thing that Martha had to go away."

Gran nodded. "We never know how strong a candle's beam may be until we try it in the dark."

Peter walked jauntily up the road that afternoon, thinking that the next two months and more were his to do with as he liked. Free time made him feel like a man, and the challenge before him to open up the path through the woods made him want to respond with everything in him. He had already cleared a small piece, but the hour or two at his disposal each day had seemed so short with the size of the work before him that he had waited for his longer, freer days to do the more strenuous work.

The nearer part along the brook would not be difficult, he told himself; but as he began to work up the slope approaching the rock ledges, there would be a test of his skill and muscle. Exploring along the overgrown road, he had discovered several places where no cutting of brush would be required at all. The nearer he got to the mountain, the more shale there was underfoot, and in it no green growth had rooted. Once he had the shale behind him, the old road dipped down again through a belt of woodland. Here the work of clearing would have to be resumed vigorously. The distance was not more than a few hundred yards before the woods came to a halt and the abandoned orchards of the neighbor farm opened before him. Climbing one of the gnarled old trees on that first scouting trip, he had been able to see the new bearing orchards and open pastures of Green Mead Farm.

Peter smiled to himself when he realized that it was taking his father all day to do a journey that could soon be done in an hour or two, once the path was opened. His fingers hungered for the ax and his ears were eager for the sound of falling brush.

Stopping at the mailbox, Peter saw that it held a letter for him. Now the day that had already seemed overflowing with happiness had an extra supply. It was from his mother. He sat down in the tall grass by the roadside and, leaning back against the post of the mailbox, read it slowly, savoring every word.

She told him that Leonard's son had been born and described the joy she had seen in Leonard's face when the baby was placed in his arms. *Leonard will gain now, more than ever,* Martha added, *and I'm glad to be here to watch the two of them put on strength and to help young Ellen with the baby.*

"Now she'll never want to come home!" Peter exclaimed, but the thought did not make him unhappy. He almost wanted her not to come back until he had completed his work on clearing the path.

There seemed to be an endless amount of time to the afternoon. Peter went to the house to drop off his books and get a glass of cold milk, then he rolled on the grass with Shep and Dusty tumbling around him, and finally he went to see the hens. Opening the little door that led from their house into the field beside the barn where they loved to scratch, Peter called to them by name.

They came through the door one by one, looking up at him, then scuttling into the field, taking hurried steps and quick leaps after elusive grasshoppers, stopping often to scratch determinedly at the ground.

"Come on, Squawker," Peter leaned down and called through the open door.

No hen appeared so Peter went into the hen house by the other door.

Squawker looked up at him from the floor. She tried to flutter toward him but, lacking the strength, fell in a heap of limp feathers. Her head drooped piteously and a film spread over her eyes; then she opened her eyes and struggled gallantly to her feet. Her bill gaped wide, but no sound came from it.

"Oh, Squawker." Peter knelt on the floor beside her, longing to do something to relieve her suffering, to give her courage in the lone battle she was fighting.

He reached out and stroked her gently and Squawker relaxed under his touch. Peter's heart was heavy. Everything within him wanted to care for the hen, but he knew instinctively that there was little one could do. Had Andrew been home there would have been one course of action he would have pursued; now, in his father's absence, Peter felt that he must do his best to act for him. It was for the good of the flock as a whole; for the good of them all. He would find Benj and then he would take Squawker to Benj. Benj would put her out of her suffering, and while he was doing that Peter would clean the hen house and put fresh shavings on the floor so the other hens would be safe against any spread of disease.

Peter moved his hands tenderly over the limp bundle of feathers, but his teeth were clenched hard. He got up to get a handful of corn from the feed bin, then he put it down in front of Squawker.

She tried to peck at it to show her gratitude, but the white film came across her eyes again and one kernel of corn was all she could manage to take in her bill.

"It's all right, Squawker. Don't be afraid. I'll get Benj."

Outside the hen house, Peter cupped his hands to his lips and called Benj's name. There was no easy answering shout so he called again. "Benj! Oh, *Benj!*"

Then he remembered. Benj was with his father on the journey to Green Mead. With a sinking heart, Peter wondered what he should do. He knew what Benj would have done, with hands as quick as they were tender; but he did not know whether he could do it, even though the edge on his ax was sharpened every night for his work in the woods.

Mary was standing on the doorstep of the house. She must have heard him call Benj's name for she had turned. Seeing Peter standing near the hen house, she started toward him.

"Peter," she said, "Granny sent me up to find out what we should feed the puppy. She thought—" Then Mary stopped short at the sight of Peter's face. "Why, Peter, what's the matter?"

He told her about the hen. "I used to think Blondie was my favorite. I used to think I couldn't bear it if anything ever happened to her, but I guess—I guess—I love Squawker a whole lot too."

"Perhaps I could take her down to Granny."

Peter shook his head. "It wouldn't be right. Not now. Not when there's been disease in the flocks. Father says there's only one thing to do with a sick hen, but Squawker isn't just a hen. She—she's my friend."

Mary went toward the hen house and opened the door quietly, speaking in low tones as she entered. A moment or two later she came out again and put her hand on Peter's shoulder. She was pale and there were tears in her eyes.

"Oh, Peter, come. Please don't mind what you see. It's really wonderful in a way."

Together they went into the hen house. There on the floor was Squawker, her legs folded under her as if she were laying an egg, her bill tucked down into her breast feathers, her eyes closed. She looked composed and settled.

Peter and Mary knelt down on the shavings beside her.

"She's been taken care of," Peter said.

"Yes," Mary whispered, as if she did not want to break the silence that had come into the hen house.

Peter felt so full of thankfulness that he brushed his sleeve across his eyes. There were the kernels of corn still before the hen.

"How peaceful she is," Mary said softly.

Peter nodded. "So be it," he murmured, thinking what Benj had said about the puppy who had come into the world unable to respond to life.

Peter picked Squawker up and wrapped her in a piece of burlap, then he placed the bundle in the wheelbarrow with a spade and a small bag of lime. Together with Mary, he went to the orchard. At the base of a young apple tree he dug a shallow grave. Shep and Dusty followed, sitting at a respectful distance. Whenever Dusty showed signs of play, Shep restrained him with a low sound in her throat. Peter placed the burlap bundle in the grave. Mary scattered the lime over it, then Peter replaced the earth, tamping it down gently.

There was no need to speak, but the air was not silent. A bluebird sang in the tree above them, telling the world of the nest with its five bluish-white eggs, telling his mate what she best understood. Swallows swirled and darted, their wings cutting the air, their ecstatic murmuring part of the fulfillment of the summer day. Peter and Mary walked back to the house together. At the doorway Peter remembered to tell her what to feed the puppy, and when. Then they said good-by.

"See you soon," she called.

"Soon," Peter echoed, waving to her as she ran across the field.

He could see the cows coming toward the barn from the pasture, a slowly moving patient line, ready to be milked. Peter went to the barn and opened the door for them. One after another, until all six had entered, they came in and found their separate stalls. Quietly they began munching at the hay that had been put there for them. Peter brought his stool and pail and started in on the milking.

It made him feel good to sit down and put his head against the warm flank of one of the cows. Working gently and speaking softly, he started the flow of milk that came noisily into the empty pail, then with a silent swish as the pail filled, foaming as it got near the top.

There was still an ache in his heart about the death of the hen, but there was something else. Something bigger than the ache, something that was comforting him. It was hard to figure it out, he thought, and it would have been harder still to explain, but even though one hen had gone, there was just as much life in the world. It was as if a curtain had been drawn down across the sun for a little minute and the light had been cut off; but when the curtain went back again, there was the light.

Picking up two brimming pails of milk, he carried them to the cool cellar. Ordinarily they felt heavy and he often slopped milk over the edges, but today he carried them easily and steadily. That was what his mother used to say comfort was: something that made you feel strong.

After a while he let the cows out to pasture, then went into the house to get his own supper and feed Shep and Dusty.

It was almost dark when Andrew and Benj returned. Benj was tired and soon went to his bed, but though Andrew was tired too, he was full of talk about his day at Green Mead and he was glad to have Peter to talk to.

"From what the herdsman says," his father explained, "they're as interested in my cows as I am in theirs. The more we can get together, the better it's going to be for both our farms."

"Did they like the pups?"

"They did and they wanted to keep them both. The farm manager wrote out a check for me while I was there. It was for more than I ever thought those pups would be worth. Shep, you've done your share to help the farm," Andrew said, stroking the dog appreciatively.

Shep looked as if she were pleased that her young had been able to take their place in the world.

Peter told his father of the hen; how the end had come to her quietly in the hen house; how he and Mary had buried her in the orchard.

His father listened without comment, then he nodded slowly. "You did the right thing," he said.

"I used to think Blondie was my favorite," Peter confessed, "but maybe they all are."

"It's not good to let yourself have any favorites on a farm," his father reminded him. "The creatures all have their work to do and their span allotted to do it in." He looked at his son, proud of the way he was proving himself able to face the challenges that came to him.

7 The Opening Path

Every afternoon, when Andrew could spare him from the work of the farm, Peter took his tools and went to the woods. An ax and a hatchet were the most used, but he carried a brush cutter also to open a way through the heavy thickets of the young alder. Shep went with him, but with authority she forbade Dusty to accompany them. She seemed to feel that Peter was her special charge and that Dusty might as well learn from the start that the house and the farm buildings were his.

During the first few days Peter slashed through a hundred yards and opened up the trail on the level land alongside the brook. He would cut for an hour and then spend the next half-hour dragging the brush into a series of piles that would be burned at the first rainy spell. He worked vigorously, hacking into the young growth, chopping at the saplings, always making his cuts as close to the ground as possible. Pausing to wipe his face and rest his arms, he would be as gratified by the light he was letting into the woodland as he was by the hard swelling of his upper right arm when he flexed it.

Alder shoots and young trees were easy to clear away compared to the greedy growth of juniper that in places had taken over a whole area, fanning out with huge prickly arms that defied a grip and often left Peter with a mass of almost invisible needles pricking his hands. One juniper was so widespread and deep-rooted that it took Peter all of the time he had in that one day to get it out and pile it for burning.

Beyond the juniper were some twenty feet where no growth had taken hold because of the underlying rock. Moss and lichens were there and a few clumps of steeplebush coming into flower. This section had been able to resist the intrusion of the woodland, and was an actual part of the old road. There was a slight rise to it. Soon Peter saw that he would be approaching the rock ledges. The hardest work of all lay before him, but once it was done the going would be easier. Perhaps by then his father would be able to help him. He longed to hear the ringing of Andrew's ax beside him in the stillness and to feel the near presence of someone other than Shep; but he longed, too, to accomplish as much as he possibly could by himself.

They were all making their contribution to the farm: Shep with her puppies; the cows with their milk; Benj with his wisdom; Andrew in the long hours of hard work that often began before the sun was up and did not cease until it dropped behind the hills in the west; even Martha, at a distance, as she enfolded the farm in her thoughts. Peter saw the opening of the path in the woods as his contribution.

The month of July was strong with heat, heat that gave impetus to growth before it began to take a toll from the land. One evening when Peter looked at the garden, he was startled by the change that had taken place in it since the morning. He felt sure that if he could watch long enough he could see the beans growing, and the corn. But other things were thriving too, and he was often kept busy with Benj, weeding between the rows and dusting the young plants against the ravages of insects.

They were able to get the hay in without any trouble from rain. The fields where it had waved tall and green looked bare and the sun burned the stubble to a dull yellow; but the barn was full of the fragrance of the new crop for days afterward. Peter's father looked at it with pride that the winter's supply of food for his stock was well stored. Still no rain came, and Andrew began to look at the drying pastures with anxiety. By the end of the month he was not the only farmer who had begun to shake his head and stare at the sky, searching it for a sign of rain. Three weeks had passed without a drop of rain falling and there was little or no dew at night. It had been good while they were haying, but now it was no longer good. The vegetables in the garden, the crops in the fields, the grass in the pasture—all had the will to grow, but without rain, roots lacked the impetus and growth was at a standstill.

Now, in the early evening when the air had cooled by a few degrees, Peter would carry pails of water from the trough in the barnyard and dole it out in the garden where it was most needed; then he would go into the woodshed and sharpen his ax for the next day's work in the woods.

Though Andrew had not yet been able to join him with the clearing, he followed Peter's progress enthusiastically. One evening Peter told his father that he was approaching the rock ledges. Andrew smiled approval that Peter had cut through so much.

"That's a rough piece of woodland," he added, "between the brook and the back side of the mountain."

"The drought's helping me, Father. There's less sap in the underbrush and it's falling to the ax more easily every day."

Benj was sitting in the doorway, letting the coolness of the evening wash over him after the heat of the day. "That's a farmer's life," he said in the way he had of speaking to no one in particular. "What's hard in one place helps in another."

"Don't be reckless when you come to the ledges," Andrew cautioned.

"I won't. They're not slippery, really. A cow could walk over that shale as well as I can."

"Maybe they're not slippery," his father said with a smile. "But a look at your trousers makes me think you've taken more than one slide."

Peter laughed and ran his hands across his knees.

"There's nothing for a boy to fear from a few rocks," Benj said, "but there might be from what lives in the rocks."

Andrew turned to him. "Are you still thinking about the rattlers, Benj?"

"I am, Andrew, and like as not the dry weather is as hard on them as it is on the rest of us."

A chill went through Peter, the only cool thing he had felt in the long hot day.

When Benj left them to go to bed, his father said, "Benj is getting old. He likes to remember the days when life was harder than it is now, and there was more danger."

Peter watched the retreating figure of Benj, thin and stooped by the years. He looked up at his father, tall and scornful of danger. "Even if there are rattlers," Peter said, "we could probably clean them out."

"I've no doubt about that. Let me know if you see or hear anything suspicious. I'll go up with you and have a look at the old den."

Another week passed without rain. Returning from his work late one afternoon, Peter stopped in the barnyard to wash his hot face with water from the trough. Then he filled two pails with water and started toward the vegetable garden.

Andrew called to him, "Easy on the water, Peter."

"But, Father, if I didn't give the vegetables some I doubt if they'd grow at all."

"This had better be the last time you water them for a while."

"Mother will be terribly disappointed if she gets back and finds her garden all burned up."

"She'd rather lose the vegetables than have the cows suffer."

"Why, what do you mean? What has happened?"

"The spring in the pasture went dry today," Andrew said. "We'll soon have to be toting water from the brook."

"The brook!" Peter exclaimed. "But even it is only half its size." He furrowed his brow. Never before had water been such a problem to them. He looked down at the two pails he was carrying. "I'll use this very carefully," he said, "and then the garden will have to take care of itself."

Peter portioned the water out to spreading squash and thriving melon. The root vegetables were not badly off and it was no use giving any to the lettuce. The hot dry weather had already made it bitter, and the shaggy wilted heads were good only to be thrown to the chickens.

When Peter returned the pails to their place beside the trough, he sloshed more water over his face, but this time he was careful to let it fall back into the trough. Benj came up to get a drink from the pump, taking the water sparingly and rolling it around in his mouth before he swallowed it.

"What's to become of the garden, Benj, unless it rains soon? Father says no more water can be spared for it."

"Aye," Benj nodded his head, "I'm not surprised. Not a quarter inch of rain did we have in July, and here we are going into August."

"But the garden, Benj, my mother's garden?"

"There isn't a plant in the garden that hasn't got roots and plenty of them," Benj said stoutly. "They may have to reach deep, but they'll hold on. There may not be the harvest we hoped for, but there'll be a harvest."

"Benj," Peter said, "do you really think there are any rattlers left on the rock ledges?"

"I've heard them on still nights, Peter," Benj answered soberly, "and once you've heard their sound you can never mistake it."

"Are they as evil as people say they are?"

"They've got no good in them for man or beast," Benj said, "but they'll not harm you if you don't first harm them."

"Have you ever seen one, Benj?"

"Seen a rattler?" The old man smiled and his blue eyes flashed their own peculiar sunshine. "There was a time when I was up on those ledges and I heard a whole chorus of them, all rattling together and in different keys. It was a wonderful thing."

"Wonderful!" Peter exclaimed. "How can anything that's deadly be wonderful?"

"They were doing no more than warning me to stay away from their little ones; so I tipped my cap and said 'Thank you kindly' and went back the way I had come."

"Father says the rattlers were cleaned out years ago."

"And perhaps they were," Benj admitted, but he shook his head as if he leaned on the side of doubt. "Just the same, tread easy and keep your eyes wide open."

It was hard to reconcile Benj's wariness with his father's assurance, Peter thought, but instinctively he sided with his father. There were so many things Benj might be hearing that might sound like rattlers singing—the wind in high branches or the brook slipping over its stones. Almost any sound could be adjusted to match the remembered sound which he had heard long ago.

Day after day the drought took its toll, searing the crops in the fields, drying the pastures, hardening the earth. The hens laid fewer eggs; the cows gave less milk; even the tempers of people began to strain; but Martha's letters coming to either Andrew or Peter every few days brought their own refreshment. Now the calendar that hung on the kitchen wall had some significance. The next leaf that turned would see her back with them. "September," she had said. The word sang in Andrew's heart and echoed in Peter's.

One evening, a cow that should have had milk in her bag came back from pasture as dry as if she had already been milked. Peter's father was puzzled, because the cattle were not dependent on the grass in the pastures but were feeding well on the corn and grain he kept in the barn for them. The next day another cow came home almost as dry as the first. The following morning, when the cows went to pasture, Andrew went with them to try to find out what was happening.

He took his seat in the shelter of a granite boulder, watching the cows at a distance.

Before noon had come, Andrew saw two half-grown fawns step daintily out of the woods and mingle with the cows as it they belonged to the herd. The cows accepted them, though a doe stood on the edge of the woods, anxious and alert. The fawns moved among the cows and first one, then the other, sought a full udder.

Andrew told Peter about it that night. "Even the feed in the forest must be getting low," he commented, "and the doe hasn't enough milk in her for her young so she sent them where they could find some. Milk tastes alike to any hungry young thing."

"You're not going to stop the fawns from feeding are you, Father?"

"No, not if they're that hungry and the cows are willing, but I hope it won't be for long."

Even Shep and her gangling pup fell under the spell of the hot weary dryness that had the land in its grip. In the daytime they dug holes for themselves under the lilac bushes, seeking some coolness in which to lie; in the evening they played slow-moving games on the doorstep, matching mouths with each other and rolling off into the grass in a tumble of fur and a flurry of meaningless growls. Their games did not last long and soon they came back to sleep on the cool earth, sinking their long noses down between their paws and rolling their eyes upward as if trying to find an answer to the question perplexing everyone.

Only Benj seemed not to be worn down by the weather; perhaps because he was older and asked less of life; perhaps because he had seen so many seasons—dry, wet, and mid-dling—and he knew that sometime the year would right itself and all would be well again.

Every evening Benj made the rounds of the place to see that the stock was all cared for, that gates that should be shut were bolted securely, that the hens were on their roost so that no misguided, wandering one would offer herself as a meal for skunk or fox before morning. Then he would go and stand at the edge of the vegetable garden, letting his eyes move up and down the rows, glad that the breath of evening had caused the chard that had wilted under the sun to stand up again and brought some revival to the huge drooping leaves of the squash. Up and down the spaces between the rows he would walk to see where fruit was forming. He felt a measure of gratitude that life was still holding on though there was small sign of any growing. If they could wait with patience through today and tomorrow, through a week of such days and maybe more, then the rain would come and with it the upsurge of growth.

A few moments later, joining Andrew and Peter in the house, he said quietly, "The corn is tasseling."

Andrew made no comment.

Peter looked up from his book. "Will we be having some corn this year, Benj?"

"We'll have a bit of everything if we can wait long enough for it."

Shep walked across the room and stood by Benj. He put his hand on her head and rubbed behind her ears with a rhythm the dog loved and had come to expect. Then Shep went over to Peter and stood beside him. He laid his hand on her gently. She meant more to him than he could ever tell anyone. Of her own will, she had chosen to spend her days with him in the woods rather than in comfort around the home place. She could do little to break the silence in which Peter worked, but she shared the loneliness with him. Peter was happy with her company. As she lay on the ground a few feet from where he was cutting and chopping, Shep's ears were ever alert, her nose always keen. Though the dryness of the season had dulled the usual scents that quickened her nostrils and tensed her ears, still the alertness was always there.

Peter stroked her. "Well, the weather is helping Shep and me," he said casually, for the lack of growth had affected many of the farm jobs that were his special charge. During the last few weeks he had been spared almost entirely from his chores. If the drought held another week, giving him that much more time, he felt that he might get through to the abandoned orchards of Green Mead Farm.

"What beans as there are should be picked tomorrow," Benj announced.

Andrew looked up at Peter. "You'll help Benj with the picking, Peter."

"Yes, Father."

"However many you get, take most of them down to Gran. She'll be able to use what we can't, without Martha."

"I've got another crop coming along that should be ready for Martha in September," Benj said.

"Can you get anything to grow in this weather?" Andrew asked.

Benj shook his head. "Maybe not grow," he said, "but waiting to grow when the rain comes."

The next day Peter worked on his clearing in the morning and helped Benj pick beans in the afternoon. Benj saved out a small basketful for them to have that night for their supper; the rest he packed into a bag which Peter carried on his back down to the valley.

It was good to see Gran. She had a glass of cool lemonade for him and a plate of cookies and, what was always as welcome, a listening ear for all he had to tell her.

"Where's Mary?"

"Gone blueberrying with Sue, but what they find won't be fit to put into a pie if I know anything about dry summers!"

"Where have they gone?"

"Back of the mountain. Mary says you've opened up the old road in good style."

Peter told her about his work. "I'm almost through to the Green Mead line." He ate another cookie. Now that most of the work was behind him it didn't seem that it had been so hard.

"You must have a lot of brush to burn."

"Sixteen good piles so far, but I'll be wanting rain for the burning."

"You're not the only one wanting rain."

Peter stayed to help with some odd chores around the place, and when he started home it was with three new baked loaves in the bag on his back and a cake in a box that he carried carefully by hand. As he went up the road, he waved to Mary and Sue, who were walking slowly over a cut field. They changed their course and came toward him.

"Get many?" he called.

Mary swung her pail in answer. Had it been even half full she would not have treated it so lightly.

"Thanks for your path, Peter," Mary said when they reached him. "We followed it through to the end of your clearing, then we went on up to the ledges."

"Plenty of blueberry bushes up that way."

"But not plenty of berries," Sue said with a laugh.

"Don't you get lonely working up there all by yourself, day after day?" Mary asked.

"Shep keeps me company, but it is awfully quiet."

"Quiet!" Sue exclaimed. "I've never heard so many cicadas in my life. Sometimes Mary and I could hardly hear each other speak."

"Cicadas?" Peter asked, looking from Mary to Sue and back to Mary.

They nodded their heads.

"I've never heard any," Peter said.

"Maybe you don't take time to listen."

Peter was still puzzled. There were many moments when he sat down to rest, leaning back against a tree, easing his arms, cooling off. At such times he was intensely aware of the silence in the woods and was glad of the sliver of sound made by the brook and of Shep's even breathing as she lay on the ground beside him.

"Cicadas are a sign of hot weather," he said.

"I wish something would be a sign of rain!" Sue exclaimed.

"When will you finish your clearing?" Mary asked.

"Tomorrow," Peter said, and then he repeated the word as if to assure himself. "Maybe tomorrow."

8 Not for the Faint-hearted

The next morning Andrew left soon after sunrise for his weekly trip to the market town. Loaded in the truck were a young bull calf, several dozen pullets in crates, and three ram lambs which he had brought down from their pasture. Benj and Peter watched him go, each of them hoping that Andrew would meet with good prices and fair bargaining.

"I can take care of the place, Peter, and do your chores too if you want to get to the woods to go on with your work," said Benj.

Peter beamed at him. "Oh, thanks, Benj. I'll put a sandwich in my pocket and not come home until it's time for the milking."

Benj chuckled. "Guess I can handle six cows if you don't get home, but it would be sociable to have you back by then."

"I'll get through to the rock ledges sure, with most of the day to work in," Peter said gleefully, "and then the toughest part will be behind me."

Peter went to the shed for his tools. He stopped by the pump in the barnyard to get a drink of water. Shep put her front paws on the edge of the trough and lapped the water thirstily.

Benj came up to him. "You're taking the dog, aren't you?"

"Oh, yes, she's my helper. She always goes with me."

"They'll rattle more if they get wind of her," Benj said, "then you'll know where not to go."

"Oh, Benj," Peter said laughing, "I don't think there are any rattlers on those ledges. I've never seen a sign or heard a sound of them."

"You haven't trespassed yet on their territory," Benj said guardedly. "They travel down to the brook to feed and may cross your path now that you're near their den." He smiled reassuringly. "But they never fail to warn, and when you hear that sound, see that you don't fail to keep your distance."

"What is their sound like?"

"Like a cicada singing," Benj said.

"Like a cicada singing!" Peter exclaimed.

"Or many of them," Benj answered. "They make sweet enough music with their tails, but they've got powerful venom in their fangs."

A chill went down Peter's spine. He shivered, standing there by the trough in the heat of the barnyard and the blazing light of the sun. "I guess I can keep out of their way," he said, conscious that his heart was beating quickly and that his words were keeping time with it. "But, Benj, why do they have that venom if it isn't any good?"

"It's their defense, Peter, and their means of obtaining food. They've got just as much right to use it as a porcupine its tail or a skunk its scent."

"Benj," Peter asked, "if—just if—Shep got too near one and it struck her, what would I do?"

"You'd have to work fast to get the venom out."

"How fast, Benj?"

Benj shook his head. "I've seen a rabbit that was struck by a rattler's fangs dead within the minute."

"What would I do, Benj, to get the venom out?"

"You'd cut the place open just as quick as ever you could and draw it out."

Peter shivered again, part in fear, part with fascination. He began to want to see a rattler at a safe distance. He began to think that it would be a dull day if he didn't have some rattling tale to bring back to Benj.

"Do you carry a knife?" Benj asked.

Peter thrust his hand into his pocket. "I do. It's the one you gave me when I was ten years old."

Benj smiled. "Sometimes a knife can be man's best friend."

Peter said good-by and walked off carrying his gear, with Shep trotting beside him. It always made him feel inches taller when Benj referred to him as a man.

"Hi, Shep," Peter said, but it was too hot to run a race across the field that morning.

Shep wagged her tail and walked close enough to Peter so he could drop his free hand to rest on her neck.

It was good to have her with him, Peter thought. As his work on the path took him farther from the open fields and nearer the rock ledges, he was increasingly glad of her company. He liked having someone to talk with, and Shep was almost as good as a person. She had her own way of taking part in conversation with the movements of her tail and the pricking of her ears. Sometimes the way she lifted her nose began the conversation that Peter carried on. Sometimes he began it with a series of rambling questions.

Leaving the field, he felt like a king as he walked along the clearing his own hand had made, past the brush piles, over the cut land, which showed in places that it had once been a road and now proclaimed that it was on the way to being one again. The day was still and warm. No breath of wind moved the trees that bordered one side of the path, and the brook bordering the other made only a whisper of sound.

When they reached the end of the cleared space, Peter placed his tools on the ground, took off his shirt, and wrapped his sandwich in it, and laid it on the earth.

"Shep," he said, "this is where you stay. Cool yourself in the brook whenever you want but always come back here and *stay* here. I'll come back to you after I get some cutting done, but I don't want you coming up behind me and getting in the way of my ax. Understand?" He pointed to the place on the ground where the shadow of a maple fell and where he had laid his extra equipment. Again he said the word "Stay" carefully and clearly.

Shep wagged her tail, then she turned away from Peter and went toward the brook.

Peter watched her for a moment as she walked in the brook, cooling the pads of her feet in the water and lowering her head to drink. Then he picked up his brush cutter and started in on the crowded growth of young alders that stood in his way. Shep returned to lie down in the place Peter had indicated was hers. Her ears were laid back, her eyes were half closed, but she did not sink her long nose between her paws. She would not let herself sleep. She was there to keep watch over Peter's belongings.

Peter thrust his tool in at the base of a clump of alders, and one after another the straggly growth with green leaves edged with brown from the summer's heat fell before him. Every few minutes he dragged the brush away to give himself clearance for cutting. Some of it he stacked in a pile for burning; a certain amount of it he layered along parallel to the path to make a break at the edge of the clearing that would discourage the woodland from crowding in another year. It was slow work, and hard. He stopped often to mop his brow, then he swung back into his work again with determination.

An hour of such work saw only a few yards cleared. Some maple saplings stood in the way now and a massive clump of juniper. He laid down his brush cutter and went back to get his ax. Leaning over to stroke Shep, he talked with her for a minute and then returned to his work.

The ground was rising perceptibly, and as the level changed, it seemed to make the cutting easier.

"At least we're getting near our goal," he called back to Shep.

More and more rocks underlaid the land as he approached the ledges. Peter stopped to survey his work. The part he had opened looked raw. Sap that was oozing from stumps dried quickly in the hot sun. A curious aroma hung over the area. Peter sniffed it, wrinkling his nose. It was the drying sap, just as he had smelled all through the summer, and yet it was different. Bitter. Acrid. He looked around him curiously, then he laughed aloud to break the silence. Of course, the air was full of the smell of the sap.

The natural pangs of hunger determined his lunchtime. When he decided to stop work and checked with the sun to see what time it was, he was surprised to find how close to noon hunger had brought him. Benj had often said that a man's own stomach was as good a clock as could be found. Peter discovered its accuracy during the days he worked alone with no reminder of time but his own needs.

Putting down his ax, he went back to Shep to collect his belongings. He pulled on his shirt and moved his tools to where he had ended his morning's work. Shep followed him. Peter made a new base near a pine tree that had grown enormous and gave a great canopy of shade. Though the air was still, the pine seemed to have caught something from the brook and the merest whisper of sound moved above them in its branches.

Before he started to eat his sandwich, Peter flattened himself on the ground by the brook and drank long and slowly, sinking his face and letting the water ripple over it; then he sat on the warm earth in a thick carpet of pine needles and leaned his back against the tree, stretching his feet out before him. Shep, seeing that he would stay as he was for a reasonable length of time, sat down beside him. She lowered her body alongside his thighs and legs, and turned her head to rest her nose across his ankles. With her body she conveyed the idea of rest and comfort, but her ears spoke alertness and her eyes were watchful.

Peter was aware again of the curious smell that came from the underbrush. It seemed so much more acrid than the drying sap that it puzzled him, though it did not seem to disturb Shep. He hoped he would remember to ask Benj about it when he got back that afternoon. Peter ate his sandwich slowly. He broke off part of the crust to give to Shep. She ate it, not so much in hunger but with the relish that comes of sharing. Peter settled back more comfortably against the tree and closed his eyes.

"Go to sleep, Shep; I'm going to for a while," he said drowsily.

Shep pricked her ears. No sound had attracted her keen hearing; no scent had crossed her sensitive nose; but she was too much the self-appointed guardian to trust the depth and distance of the woods. Her master might take his ease, but she would remain on guard. Though the August day was warm and the woods were full of quiet, and the slipping of the brook over its stones was murmurous with peace, Shep would not close her eyes. Peter's hand that had been resting on her back fell away. Shep turned to him, missing the slight pressure of the familiar; then, when she saw that Peter's eyes were closed and his lips made no sound, she turned her head back again to watch.

The summer day moved on. High up in the trees a light soughing of wind stirred among the branches. Insects droned in measureless music that quickened, then lapsed again into casual minstrelsy. Far away a lowing came from the cows in the Green Mead pastures. All along the treeless side of the mountain, the heat of the sun quivered on shale slope and rock ledges. Small flecks of mica splintered in the rock caught the sun and flashed it back, making the rugged slope look like a glittering mosaic.

Slowly, leisurely, as if endless time attended every move, a coiled form on one of the rock ledges unwound itself, lifting its heart-shaped head to the sun. Looking around and waving a small forked tongue to test the air, the snake made a series of undulations. But it was not the sun that had wakened it, for under that rain of heat it might have slumbered on. It was a need far down within it, a pang of hunger that reverberated through the body, knocked within the head, and brought instinctive response.

The tongue waved again in the air, but the air brought no promise of warm-blooded food at hand. The dark form with its banded scales gleaming like dull sulphur drew itself together, then lengthened out again, sidling cautiously down the slope. Over the shale it went, then over rock so pleasurable with its warmth that the snake lingered for a moment, twisting its body in quick movements. Then, gliding more swiftly, it went across moss and decaying leaves to the brook. Coiled into its attitude of expectancy, the snake waited until some hapless mouse or lightly leaping frog might offer itself as food.

The day dreamed on. A tired boy slept and a faithful dog shifted with uneasiness, trying to nudge the boy into waking. On the rock ledge another form uncoiled and slid slowly down toward the water, passing on the way its gorged and surfeited mate. They lifted their tails, each recognizing the presence of the other; lidless eyes gazed coolly, then the one with bulging sides moved up the slope while the other went toward the brook.

Peter woke with a start, though once awake he could not have said what had roused him. "Hello, Shep," he mumbled, glad to feel the dog's body pressed close against him. "What time is it?"

Shep flapped her tail and stood up, stretching and shaking herself.

"Time to get up," Peter said, supplying the words for her. He rubbed his eyes and got clumsily to his feet. Momentarily stiff-muscled, he stood for a moment blinking, stretching his arms above him and letting some of the sleepiness out of him in a loud rasping yawn.

There was a sound in the underbrush, hollow, fearsome, sinister. It was repeated distantly.

Peter stiffened. Instantly everything within him came awake. "Like a cicada singing!" The words slipped through his mind, galvanizing him to action.

Shep pounced quickly on something moving through the leaves, but even her speed was slow compared to that of the snake, which doubled its length in the distance it put between itself and the dog before Shep's nose could pick up its scent again.

Regaining the rock ledges, the snake rattled stridently until the whole of the mountain slope seemed to reverberate with sound.

"Shep!" Peter cried.

Shep was not to be stopped. Picking up the scent, she wove back and forth along it, flinging herself through the brush and onto the slippery shale.

"Shep, come back!" Peter called sternly.

In her excitement, she had gone beyond the range of his control. Maddened by the thing that had escaped her and drawn by its lure, she was incapable of obeying Peter's command. It was as if she were on a cord with the far end tucked in some cranny of the rock ledges, drawing her toward them.

Peter followed her, crashing through the underbrush, tripping over a root and picking himself up again. He was held back for a moment when his shirt caught on the dead limb of a tree. As he yanked it fiercely to free himself, the material groaned and split in protest. Racing over the shale, he was less nimble than Shep, for the pads of her feet could grip while the soles of his shoes slipped and slid.

Up to the edge of the den among the rock ledges Shep pursued the scent. There, three coiled snakes, their scaly yellow and black sides gleaming like velvet in the shade cast by an overhanging rock, gave warning with raised and singing tails that intrusion would not be tolerated. Small eyes peered from flat heads waving slowly back and forth in anger. Forked tongues darted balefully in and out. One of the three reared itself slightly, muscles tense, body poised, ready to strike.

"Shep! Shep!" Peter screamed.

Shep needed now no warning of Peter's. Seeing her quarry for what it was, she shuddered with a dog's instinctive horror of reptiles and stopped within two feet of the trio. Peter, catching up with her, threw out his hand to pull her back to him.

The snake, seeing the hand coming toward it and acting in defense, struck. It took only an instant for the wide mouth to close on the outflung arm, but only a second was needed for the fangs to loose their venom; then the snake re-coiled itself and slithered away with the others into the holes that ran down under the shale, their rattles echoing within the walls of their retreat.

Shep looked up at Peter, pleased at having routed the snakes. She wagged her tail and rubbed against him, but Peter had no eyes for Shep. He was gazing at the swelling on his arm.

The world blurred and a sickening wave came over Peter that took from him all power to think, all will to action. He swayed unsteadily. Shep, sensing that something was wrong, jumped against him and barked imperatively. Peter put his good hand on her back to steady himself. Shep barked again, insistently, impatiently, baring her teeth with urgency.

In the fog that surrounded him, Peter did not hear a dog barking. He heard an old man saying, "Cut it open, cut it open."

Peter reached into his pocket and fumbled to open his knife, using his teeth and his good hand; then, where the fangs had gone and the swelling was already turning dark, he plunged in the knife. The first spurt of blood made the faintness come over him again; so he closed his eyes that he might be able to go on with what he was doing. Through what seemed an age of time, he drew his knife along his forearm the length of the swelling. The cut made by the knife did not seem to hurt, for the raging of the venom was so much more intense.

Peter opened his eyes and looked at the wound. Red and gaping, the blood could not seem to flow freely from it, for a yellowish scum rested on the surface of the blood. He knew what it was. The thing that he had to get rid of. He pressed the sides of the wound, but that did not drive out all the venom. Closing his eyes again, he held the wound to his mouth and sucked; then he spat out all that he had drawn in. He opened his eyes and looked at the wound. It was clean now. Red blood was flowing from it like sap from a tapped maple in March. He pulled off his shirt, and where the dead limb had torn it, he tore it again and made a bandage, tying it tightly as he could above the wound to check the bleeding.

Shep watched with wondering, helpless eyes, offering the slender wall of her body as something for the boy to lean against during his sixty-second battle for survival. When the arm was bandaged, Peter laid his hands heavily on Shep's back. He was trembling violently. Pain, no longer localized in his arm, seemed to be shooting through him. Sweat beaded his face and drenched his body, making him feel desperately hot and then shivering with cold.

"Let's get away from here, Shep," he said, his voice thick and unsteady, his legs uncertain.

Putting himself in the dog's charge, he let her lead him over the shale and through the brush, across the cutting he had done that morning to the brook. Shep was as gentle as she had been many a time with a lost and bewildered lamb, and as forceful. Generations of training had made her sure of one thing—that when she took over, it was full charge or nothing.

At the brook, she placed the weight of her body against Peter until he dropped to his knees and put his face in the water. When she decided he'd had enough, she took the belt of his trousers between her teeth and shook him. Peter groaned and staggered to his feet, then fell back against the moss and stones alongside the brook. Shep sat down beside him contentedly. The boy had done what she wanted him to do. She did not care now if he sat quietly, hugging his arm against his body. Racked by pain as he was, Peter felt so drained of energy that he was powerless to move. Shep watched him anxiously, nuzzling toward him to lick his hand or his face, then barking imperatively to compel his attention.

Wind quivered through the branches of the trees high above their heads. The brook slipped over its stones at their feet. Up the slope of the mountain and deep in one of its rocky crevices, a company of snakes sang on, the sound growing less vigorous and more rhythmical until it was absorbed into the silence of the woods and the warmth of the summer day.

9 One Good Arm

The cows came up to the pasture bars for milking. Benj let them into the barnyard. One by one they went into the barn and found their own stalls. Benj lingered by the bars to look down the pasture toward the woodland. He felt uneasy about Peter. Then he chided himself for his feeling. It was a tempting thing to be near the end of a task. Peter had probably given himself another hour to complete the cutting, knowing that Benj could take care of the milking.

Dusty pushed himself against Benj's legs, whimpering.

Benj fondled him. "Wondering where your mother is, are you? Ah well, she'll be home before long and a tired lady she may be. She'll have none of your rough games until she's had her supper."

Dusty lifted his lips and tossed his head, then he capered around Benj, glad that someone understood him.

Benj went into the barn to milk the cows. With each one he had long conversations as he rested his head against a smooth flank and his knowing hands worked on until the pails were full.

"They're not giving what they should, with the sun drying up their pastures," Benj said to Dusty. "But you shall have your share." He poured some milk into a low pan and Dusty lapped delightedly.

Benj carried the pails to the cellar. He collected the eggs and tossed some grain to the hens. He let the cows out to pasture again. Then, with nothing more to do around the place, he started out across the field in the direction of the woods. Dusty frolicked around him.

Benj looked stern and pointed back to the barn. "You stay," he said. "Who's to look after the place if we all leave it?"

Dusty's ears and tail drooped.

Benj repeated the command.

Unwillingly the pup accepted his responsibility. Slowly, as if his feet were moving through tar, he went back and sat in the barn doorway.

Benj felt satisfied that Dusty knew what was expected of him, and he turned to face the fields again. It was then that he saw Peter come out of the woods, walking slowly and without his shirt on.

One arm, wrapped in something white, was held across his chest; he was dragging his tools with the other. Shep was walking close beside him.

"Peter!" Benj called from the rise of land on which he stood.

Peter looked up at the sound of Benj's voice, but he made no attempt to wave.

Benj started toward the boy. Nearing him, he saw the pallor of Peter's face and the roughly bandaged arm. Peter was breathing heavily and his forehead was beaded with sweat. Benj stood beside him, repeating his name.

"Peter," he said gently, "Peter."

Peter looked at Benj as if he did not recognize him. He felt someone standing near him, near enough so that the smell of farm clothes was real and strong. He felt a work-roughened hand rest on his shoulder; but it was not until he heard Benj speak his name a second time that the dazed look began to leave his face.

"Hello, Benj." His words had a thick sound as if he had been wakened out of sleep.

Benj searched the wan young face that usually broke with such ease into a smile.

Peter blinked his eyes; then Benj saw the smile coming like a pale sun out of a morning of mist.

Benj placed his fingers lightly on the bandaged arm. "You never did that with ax or brush cutter," he said slowly, "for it was I who taught you how to handle tools and you didn't learn from me to harm yourself."

Peter shook his head.

"And it wasn't a wild creature, for none of them would have let you off with only your shirt and a scratch on your arm."

Peter shook his head again, then he lifted his eyes and looked at Benj. As their glances met, a momentary twinkle played in Peter's eyes. "Guess again, Benj."

"It wasn't a rattler," Benj said, "or you wouldn't be here to tell the tale."

Peter smiled, but the smile turned quickly into a grimace as the pain still shooting through his arm made itself felt. He swallowed hard. "But I *am* here!" His words were stouter than the voice that uttered them.

Benj let out an exclamation. "You're not keeping it all to yourself, are you?" Reaching over, he patted Shep on the rump. "Go off to your son, he's been asking for you this last hour and more." Then he took the tools from Peter's hand and shouldered them.

Shep, willing now to be released from her duty since she could turn her charge over to one of his own kind, raced off across the field to the house.

Peter told Benj his story as they made their way slowly up the rise of land.

At the end Benj said, "If the dog had got the venom it would have killed her sure. A man is hardier." He smiled proudly at Peter. "Does the wound hurt much?"

Peter nodded his head. He could not trust his answer to words.

"That's a poor sort of bandage you've got on it, though it was a good shirt once. When I'm getting the supper you'd best go down the hill to Mary's gran and let her make you a proper bandage."

Benj helped Peter wash and put on a clean shirt. After a while Peter went down to the valley and presented himself at the door of the small stone house.

"I'm needing a proper bandage, Granny, do you think you could give me one?" he asked as she opened the door to him.

It was nothing new for Gran to be asked to dress a wounded arm. She could do a splint as well, or take a stitch in torn flesh if need be, and many of the neighborhood went to her for just such help when they had not the time or the strength to go farther down the valley to the doctor.

"Well now, what's this?" she asked as she unwound the clumsy wrapping and soaked it with warm water so it would come away from the wound without further tearing.

"A cut," Peter said, then he winced as the last piece of the shirt came off. He turned his eyes away quickly so he would not see the ugly gash in the flesh.

"And how did it happen?"

"With a knife."

"Hmm," Gran murmured. "You should be a bit more careful when you use a knife."

"I know that now," Peter replied.

She looked at him earnestly, trying to read in his eyes something his lips were reluctant to say. She bent over and smelled the wound. "It's something more than a cut," she said.

Peter was silent.

Gran began to nod her head, then she looked up at Peter, knowingly this time. "You're a brave lad, a quick-thinking lad, and that's all I'm going to say."

With deft and careful movements she washed the wound and dressed it, making a neat bandage, which she fastened securely. "The next time you look at it you'll scarcely see a scar. The young heal quickly. Mary," she called, "bring Peter some milk and a piece of gingerbread before he goes home."

Peter accepted the food gladly. He was hungry and he felt proud of the bandage Gran had given him.

"What a good thing it was your left arm," Mary commented.

Peter nodded, his mouth too full of gingerbread for him to agree in words.

"Did you finish the cutting today?"

"No, not quite," Peter said, then he grinned. "But I heard the cicadas singing, many cicadas."

When Peter left, Gran followed him to the door. "How did you get it so clean?" she asked.

"I did the only thing I could think to do," Peter answered. "I put it to my lips and sucked the venom, then I spat it out." He spoke slowly. He felt tired and his arm was aching.

Gran nodded. "That's the best way to clean such a wound, but it takes a deal of courage. Your father will be proud of you."

"Will he?" Peter smiled, feeling that if his father were proud of him, anything would have been worthwhile.

That night after supper, Peter and Benj sat on the doorstep letting the cool breath of evening take away the feel of the day's heat. Benj asked Peter again about the episode and Peter told him all that he could remember.

"I don't want to go that way again," Peter concluded.

"What way?"

Peter jerked his head toward the mountain. "Where the snakes live. Where they come down to the brook. It's a bad place over there. I don't like it."

Benj said nothing. It was almost as if he had not heard Peter, except that he nodded his head slowly. His gnarled hands opened and closed upon his knees. At length he spoke. "It's odd, Peter, but that's just the one thing we can't afford to do—give way to our fear."

"What do you mean, Benj?" Peter asked, his eyes wide and wondering.

"Somehow or other we've got to meet the challenge of fear if we do nothing else in this life," Benj said.

"I'm not afraid."

"You are if you don't want to go that way again."

Peter was silent; when he spoke it was in a voice that sounded thin and faraway. "You mean I'll go on with my cutting sometime?"

Benj nodded. "Not sometime, Peter, tomorrow. You've got one good arm, haven't you?"

"Yes, of course, I have," Peter answered quickly. "And it's my right arm too."

"It just may be, if the weather holds, that you and I and Andrew have got our work cut out for us tomorrow."

"You mean—"

"I mean we'll clean out the rattlers first and then finish the cutting."

"Oh, Benj!" Peter's face was shining, then his brow furrowed. "But the weather is going on like this forever, isn't it? I think it's forgotten how to rain."

"Did you see the sun set tonight? There was a cloud no bigger than a man's hand resting on the mountains. That was a sign in olden days and weather signs don't change. You'll feel rain on your face before many more days have passed. But I'd like to see that den of snakes cleaned out before the rain comes."

Benj had the look of a crusader in his face. In spite of his great respect for all living creatures, he knew that some could not bide too close to man and the domestic animals. The snakes might have lived out their lives, untroubling man and untroubled by him, had their den not lain near the path that connected two farms. Now, because their presence spelled disaster, they must go. Benj did not like the thought of what had to be done, but the years had made him wise.

Before Peter went up to bed he said, "Benj, will my father let me go with him to Green Mead when he leads Princess there?"

"Perhaps."

"I want him to take me with him then—so much!"

"That's distant by several days," Benj reminded him. "The work we have before us tomorrow is enough to think about now."

Benj was sitting at the kitchen table when Andrew returned. Andrew looked tired, and he sighed heavily as he sat down across from Benj and put his head in his hands.

"I don't know what I'm going to do," he said, "if I have to keep buying corn for the cattle, Benj. The drought has put the price up so high that it's almost out of an honest man's reach."

"The drought can't go on much longer, Andrew."

"No, nor can I." Andrew lifted his head and looked across the table. "Benj, sometimes I'm fearful that I may lose the farm."

There was such silence in the kitchen that the clock sounded like a smith hammering on an anvil.

"I'll not believe it, Andrew." Benj broke the silence with hearty words. "This is the land your father cleared for you and that you are bettering for your son. You'll not lose it if—"

"If?"

"If you don't lose your hold on yourself first."

Andrew accepted Benj's words. He said nothing, but his fingers clenched within his fists and all his muscles were taut.

Benj laid his hand on Andrew's shoulder. "It's not so bad as all that, Andrew. You'll find things turning for the better soon. It's like waiting for sun-up. The light comes behind the mountains in its time, no matter how long and dark the night has been. I've seen it happen too often to doubt." Benj smiled. "You don't get to be an old man for nothing. Go to bed, Andrew, and get some rest. You'll see things better in the morning."

"It's hard to sleep when there are worries in your mind."

"True, but you need your sleep tonight, Andrew. We've got a job of work to do tomorrow."

"We have?" Andrew looked at Benj in curiosity. He knew of no work ahead until rain came and gave growth to the land. There would be plenty of tasks then, but until that time most of their usual work was in abeyance.

"Aye."

"What is it?"

"Clean out a den of rattlesnakes."

Andrew let out an exclamation. His face, which had told of weariness and despair, now looked startled and intent.

"I'll say no more," Benj went on, "for I don't want to spoil the boy's story. He's been doing a man's work on that clearing, Andrew, but it will take the three of us tomorrow to do what has to be done before you'll be willing to take your best heifer over that path."

Andrew put his hand up slowly to his chin, holding it thoughtfully. He said nothing, but everything in him was giving assent. There was a manner to Benj when he was sure of anything. Andrew had never questioned him then; he knew he never would.

"All right, Benj, I'll be ready."

"Buttercup Princess should be led over to Green Mead sometime next week, Andrew," Benj said casually, as if their whole conversation had been on things of easy import.

"Next week! But Martha may be coming home then."

"True," Benj said.

"Well." Andrew paused, thinking. "I'll plan to take her whatever day you say."

"Peter could lead her over that path as well as you could."

Andrew laughed, a sharp brittle sound. "Do you think I'd trust a boy with my finest heifer?"

"You'll be trusting him with all you've got someday, Andrew. You might begin by trusting him now with one of your cows."

"Time enough to do that when he gets to be a man."

"Perhaps, but he's gone a long way to becoming a man today."

Andrew looked at Benj questioningly, but Benj did not seek his glance. Instead he pushed his chair back from the table and started out of the room.

"Good night, Andrew."

"Good night, Benj."

Benj opened the screen door and went out into the night. The door made a dull thud behind him. He stood in the darkness under the sky flecked with stars and lifted his eyes to the hills.

10 The Rim of Fire

At breakfast the next morning Peter kept his left arm in his lap. There was much to ask his father about his trip to market, and there was much to tell him about the work in the woods; but Peter felt his story could wait while he listened to his father's.

Andrew told Peter that the prices he had received for the stock he had taken with him had been offset by the prices he had had to pay for the grain he brought back with him to carry them through the dry season. "Nothing goes into the bank or my pocket from that journey," he said in conclusion.

"Benj says rain is coming."

Andrew laughed good-naturedly. "I doubt if it comes today with the sun riding as it is in a cloudless sky."

"He saw a sign last night in the sunset."

"He's always been good at signs, but I hope he isn't seeing in the sky too much of what his heart is hoping for. May I have some more milk, please, Peter?"

Peter had a spoon in his right hand, so he lifted his left from his lap to move the pitcher nearer to his father. For the first time that morning Andrew saw the bandaged arm.

"Peter, you hurt yourself yesterday!" he exclaimed, half in surprise, half in reproach.

Peter smiled, proud of the mark of his conflict, eager now to talk about it. Yesterday the telling of it to Benj had given him the same queasy feeling he had when he first saw the yellowish fluid resting on the open wound; but today was different. There was less pain now in the wound and no fear in his heart, and one arm was almost as good as the other.

"That's the adventure I had yesterday," Peter said. He put his arm back in his lap and told his father what had happened. After Shep started to get him away, it was not clear to him exactly what had taken place, he said. "But she was wonderful, Father. I felt just like one of the lambs when she gets them to safety. As soon as the brook water ran over my face I began to feel better."

"How long were you lying beside the brook?"

"I don't know."

Straight and steady, Andrew looked at his son across the table. He said nothing, but their eyes met and each saw in the other's glance something he had been hungering for.

"How many rattlers are up there?"

"I saw three. They were making such a din that I couldn't tell whether there were more or not."

"Are you sure they hole up in those crevices?"

"Yes," Peter said impulsively; then he measured his statement. "Well, as sure as one can be of anything. Why?"

"If they do, it will be easy to get them. Benj wants us to go up today and clean them out."

"How do we do that?"

Andrew shrugged his shoulders. "Benj has a way. He'll tell us what he wants us to do." Andrew laughed. "This is one day when we take our orders from him. Wear your heaviest pair of leather boots and put on a long-sleeved shirt to protect that arm."

"Yes, Father."

Long before midmorning the chores were done, the luncheon was packed, and the tools had been assembled. Peter, Andrew, and Benj were ready to start off. Much to the disgust of the two dogs, they were forbidden to accompany the men. Shep used every wile she possessed to persuade them to take her, and Dusty, in high-spirited uncertainty, did everything his mother did. But Andrew was firm.

"You stay here," he said to Shep, holding her long muzzle in his hands and gazing into her eyes.

Looking at him as if he had beaten her, she lowered herself across the doorstep and sighed. Dusty came and sat beside her.

Andrew turned and picked up his ax, then he slung the rucksack with their luncheon in it over his shoulder. In his right hand, Peter carried a covered pail with milk which they would stand in the brook to keep cool for drinking later. Benj picked up the remaining tools and a small can of kerosene.

While they were walking across the field toward the woods, Peter looked from Benj to his father, wondering why there was such silence between them. Then he realized that his father was letting Benj control the day, and there was something in Benj's face that said plainly he did not want to be disturbed, that he was thinking things out. When they came to the path Benj walked ahead of them, his keen eyes searching, searching, his ears ready to catch the slightest sound.

"Shouldn't we make some noise?" Peter asked anxiously. "Just to let them know we're coming?"

"They know already," Benj said. "The ground has been vibrating with our tread ever since we came into the woods. They'll seek the shelter of their den and that's what we want them to do."

Andrew looked from side to side of the clearing and along the open path before them. "It's a fine way you've made, Peter. We shall be able to lead cows over it easily."

Peter felt proud and grateful. One word his father had used kept singing in his mind with an echo of inner happiness. It was the little word *we*.

The level was rising now. Benj stopped still and listened, holding his hand up for quiet. He heard the sound before the others did—the distant whirring. It was little different from the wind in the trees except for its significance. As they approached the shale, they veered from the path and started to scramble up toward the rock ledges. Almost as if he were following a mark on the ground, Benj went toward the crevices in the rock side of the mountain.

Peter pointed ahead. "It's there that I saw the three yesterday."

Benj glanced around him. "There are more than three."

"How can you tell?"

"The stench," Benj said.

Peter drew in a series of short sniffing breaths. "So that's what the smell is!" he exclaimed.

Near the den there was silence, then the singing began again. It was not an angry sound, but strident, echoing from within the rock walls. Benj leaned over and looked at some tracks in the dust. He straightened up and glanced around him.

Andrew asked him the question that he had been longing to put ever since the previous night, but knowing Benj, he knew it could only come at the proper time. "What are you going to do, Benj?"

"Stuff the crevices with wood, and build a rim of fire around the area, soaking the wood with this oil I've brought. That will bring them out, and I'll take care of them myself when they come over or through the fire."

Andrew laughed. "Sounds simple."

Benj nodded. "The simple way is sometimes the best. Snakes don't like to be shut in their holes and they are cold-blooded creatures; only a few degrees of heat over and above their usual are more than their bodies can stand. They'll come up to the openings, and then they'll come out. The fire will take care of them to an extent, and my ax will do the rest."

Andrew and Benj stopped up the holes with wood, twigs, and small dry sticks that Peter brought to them. Then Benj laid more wood carefully on the shale so that a complete circle was formed around the place where the crevices were, a circle some foot or more deep.

"The country's dry to light a fire in the open," Benj remarked, "but it can't run on the shale and there's not a breath of wind to carry any embers."

He knelt down by the circle of dried wood. Peter watched in fascination. From far within the rock only the slightest whirring sound came, reverberating dully against the walls that enclosed it. The added darkness from the closing of the openings had made the rattlers feel momentarily safe.

Benj held the match in his hand for a long moment before he struck it and ignited the dry twigs. He shook his head heavily. Andrew felt sorry for Benj. He knew the respect Benj had for the ways of living things; he knew that Benj disliked depriving anything of life; but he knew, too, that when Benj had to do it, he could in the kindest, surest way.

Benj struck the match. Flame spurted and he held it to the wood. In a moment the dry kindling was crackling and flaring. Benj stepped back, away from the heat. He stood there grim and silent, thinking his own thoughts as he watched the flames eat into the wood.

"Go along now," he said to Andrew. "I'll do the rest myself."

Andrew turned away reluctantly and started across the shale, down the slope toward the brook.

Peter followed him, but he looked back more than once. All he saw was Benj standing motionless, ax in hand; all he heard was the snapping of the dry wood as smoke gave way to flame.

Twenty minutes later Benj joined them. "That's done," he said, and the tone in which he uttered the words implied that he would say no more.

Sitting by the brook, they ate their sandwiches and drank freely of the milk, then they swung into such wholehearted work as the woodland had not seen before. But Andrew would not let Peter do any cutting.

"Father, please! I'm all right, really I am."

Andrew shook his head. "I don't want you to risk opening the wound or to put your body heat up with exertion." He reached over to take the brush cutter from Peter's hands. "You'll have enough to do giving us orders and telling us how the work is going."

Peter surrendered the cutter. At least he was not to be entirely idle.

Benj chuckled as he aimed his ax at a crooked pine, felling it in a single stroke.

The speed of their progress amazed Peter when he recalled his own slow pace during the weeks he had been hacking alone at the clearing. Benj worked like a man who had shed twenty years, like a man in his prime of strength and skill. Andrew put into his chopping all the power that had gone to make the farm what it was and which he knew would save it. With his powerful arm and unerring eye, one stroke was all he needed for each young tree that stood in the path. Marching into the tangled heart of a juniper bush, he dug out its roots as if he had been told that gold lay beneath them.

Peter watched the work and gave directions, scouted ahead and came back with the news that fifty yards remained to be done, then forty, then thirty. When it got down to ten they were rewarded with the sight of an opening in the green curtain before them. Soon they cut their way out of the jungle of brush into the comparative freedom of the abandoned orchards of Green Mead Farm. They sat down to rest on a rise of land. Looking behind, they could see the work they had done; the work that was the finishing touch to Peter's lonely labor during the hot summer days. Looking before them, they could see the Green Mead cattle grazing in their wide pastures, the neat spread of barns, and all the evidences of a prosperous, well-kept dairy farm.

Andrew leaned against a tree, breathing heavily. His face was hot and flushed from the exertion of the past two hours, but the furrowed line that worry had plowed between his brows had disappeared and his eyes were shining. To Peter, the opening of the path meant the triumph of endurance and strength; but only Andrew knew what it meant to have his farm and Green Mead linked by a ribbon of road, instead of being separated by a half-day's journey around the mountain. His heifers now could be led easily to their breeding, and when his strain was improved, Green Mead would be bringing their own heifers to him.

"Even their fields are dry," Peter said.

"They'll be as glad to get the rain as we will be."

On the way back, they walked easily over the cleared path, each one eager to scramble up the rock ledge and see the results of earlier work. The fire had gone and there was only a bed of gray ash with a few blackened bits of wood in it. In the ash and scattered over the shale were the charred or mangled forms of eight rattlers of varying sizes.

"Let them be," Benj said. "The venom still has power. Only time will deaden it." He turned to Andrew. "I think there'll be no more trouble."

Andrew put his hand on Benj's shoulder. The gesture meant more than words. It was not the first time Benj had used his skill and knowledge to protect the life of the farm.

Leaving the path and starting across the field, Benj called Peter's name suddenly and pointed up to the sky. Unbelievable as it might seem, clouds were massing in the southwest.

"Clouds!" Peter exclaimed. "I'd almost forgotten what they looked like."

"There'll be rain before dark," Benj observed.

"Rain!" Andrew repeated, reverence in his tone.

Peter heard it that night after he had gone to bed, drumming on the roof, sluicing against the windowpanes, gurgling down the gutter pipe. He thought that never in his life had he heard anything more beautiful. He wanted to listen to it as he would to his mother's voice when she read aloud to him; but the steady drone had sleep in it and even while he was listening he found himself slipping off into happy oblivion.

Andrew stood by his window watching the rain splash down the panes. "It's not too late to save the land," he said to himself over and over. Matter of fact as the words were, the look on his face spoke the thankfulness in his heart.

11 News

The rain kept up through the night and into most of the next day. It was not until late afternoon that it eased off at all; then the clouds rolled back over the mountains and for a brief hour before it set, the sun shone on a world of dazzling splendor.

Every leaf, every blade of grass, held a tiny prism that reflected light. In the vegetable garden, the huge leaves of the squash and the tapering leaves of the corn caught the rain and held it in their hollows: one shimmering drop to a leaf, yet each one was enough to give back glory to the sun. In the flower garden, the petunias had been dashed to the ground, but the zinnias stood like soldiers at salute. In the pastures that had been brown and seared, a green flow of color came in the wake of the rain and the cows ate as if they were in paradise. The chickens scuttled from their house into the field, hungry for the worms and slugs that would now be near the surface. Blondie and Copper Queen flashed gleaming feathers in the light; Amazon walked among a flock of pullets as if they were all her raising.

The chores were easy that day, most of them limited to the barn. Andrew and Benj spent their time mending tools and repairing harness, and often just standing in the doorway of the barn, drinking in with their eyes the goodness that was falling on the land. Peter found a dozen excuses to do errands in the rain. He took off his shirt and his shoes, rolled his pants up to his knees, and went from house to barn, from mailbox to garden, from the hens to the cows, as if every journey were indispensable. The bandage on his arm became so soaked that he took it off, and no other was put in its place for the wound had healed and only a red mark showed where his knife had plunged.

"Benj, it won't go all away, will it?" he asked.

"Like as not."

"But I don't want it to. I want to have a scar to show my friends when I go back to school."

"When's that?"

"In just two weeks."

Benj looked at the red mark more closely. "There'll still be a little something there." He smiled into Peter's face. "But if it's proof you're wanting, I'll give you some."

"What?"

"The rattles from those eight snakes."

"Benj!"

"Aye, tomorrow maybe, or as soon as I go up that way again, I'll cut off those rattles and give them all to you."

Peter slid his hands in his pockets as if they were already full of the rattles. Nothing could have more value or be more useful to him when he got back to school. He put his head back and laughed at the prospect.

"Benj, I've never been in a hurry to get back to school, but now—but now—"

Benj nodded his head. He knew what had value too.

After supper that night, when the world was fresh and damp and still dripping and all nature seemed to be breathing new life, Benj told Andrew that they should try to get the brush piles burned the next day.

"They'll drain off enough so we can get them lighted, but no matter how much they blaze they'll not endanger the woods or the land, for everything is so wet."

Andrew agreed. Put it off a few days and more rain might come which would make the brush hopelessly sodden. Put it off and another dry spell might mean they would have to wait until winter snows came before they could burn the brush.

"It will take more than our three pairs of hands to get those piles burned," Andrew said. "How many do you think there are, Peter?"

"Twenty-one, or it may be twenty-two."

"We could make a start," Andrew said.

Peter looked toward him eagerly. "Father, why don't I get Randy to help us, and Sam and Sue might come, and maybe

Mary and Gran? There's not so much work to the burning, just the watching and turning the butt ends in."

"If you could get them," Andrew said, "the work might get done between noon and nightfall tomorrow."

First thing the next morning Peter raced down the hill to ask his friends to come up and help them burn brush. Mary was excited at the thought. She looked longingly at her grandmother.

"Won't you come too, just for a little while?"

Gran laughed. "Time was when I could tend a brush pile as well as any man, but now I do other tending. You go along, Mary, and I'll come up in the late afternoon with some supper for you all."

Soon after luncheon, the clearing along the brook was resounding with the shouts and laughter of Peter and his friends, the strong voices of Andrew and Benj, and the crackling of flames from the many brush piles. Lining the path at regular intervals the piles stood. One would be set alight by Andrew or Benj, then another, and so on down the long line. Columns of smoke rose up from the green wet wood, sputtering and fuming, but soon the intense heat ate into the branches and leaves, and the smoke changed to roaring pillars of fire that shot high up to the sky.

When the fires were all blazing well, the seven people were each assigned three piles to watch. With rakes and long-handled pitchforks they kept turning the unburned outer pieces into the roaring center, gradually closing in the area of burning so that as the fire burned itself out only a wide circle of warm white ash was left and in the very center a glowing bed of coals.

Faces were seared with the heat. Bare arms were covered with ash and small flecks of blackened wood that sailed into the air and then came down to settle where they would. But voices rang high and flames gradually dropped. By late afternoon there were twenty-one circles of cooling ash to mark where the brush piles had stood. Andrew and Benj raked over the circles until every charred log that had been livid and quivering was reduced to embers, and then the embers themselves gradually went out.

Gran had seen the columns of smoke and she had judged her time well, starting out across the fields when she knew the heaviest part of the work would have been accounted for and appetites would be as sharp as the edge on a woodsman's ax.

Randy had just come up from the brook where he had been trying to wash his soot-blackened hands and arms when he saw Gran coming, dragging behind her a small cart piled high with baskets.

"Look, Mary! Look, Peter!" he shouted.

Sam and Sue came running. Andrew rested on his rake. Mary went toward her grandmother to welcome her. The others stood watching. Benj took that moment to slip away from them, mounting slowly up the shale incline to the ledges. There was a smile on his face and his fingers were feeling in his pocket for his knife.

That was a supper to be remembered. They sat around the biggest of the fires, which still had gleaming coals in its center. Gran had brought potatoes to roast in the coals and bacon for them to broil on sticks. She had brought a pot of coffee for herself and Andrew and Benj. There was a pail of milk cooling in the brook, which Andrew had brought down with him after he had gone back to the farm to do the milking. There were new-made rolls and tomatoes from the garden, huge and juicy and warm from the sun.

After they had eaten everything and thought they could not possibly eat any more, there was still a basket left in the cart, a flat basket with a cover on it and a little latch that held the cover in place.

Mary went to the cart and came back with the basket. "I think I can guess what it is," she said.

"Put it before Peter's father," Gran said. "It's got his name on it."

Mary put the basket down on the ground. "Three guesses," she challenged him.

"I know what it is," he said, "but not what's in it—unless—unless—" He opened the basket and took out the largest pie any of them had ever seen.

"Oh! Ohhh!" Sam and Randy and Peter shouted, knowing then that they were not really so full as they had thought they were a few minutes ago.

Mary clapped her hands over her mouth so that she would not let out the secret of what was in the pie, and Sue stood still and waited expectantly.

In the center of the pie, where the little steam vent was usually slashed, a big *A* looked up at Andrew. Its edges were spattered with tiny specks of red from the bubbling that had gone on inside.

Andrew looked at Gran. "It's cherry pie."

She nodded. "From the very tree you used to raid when you were a boy," Gran said tartly, "but you never took them quite all. I could always manage a pie or two every season." She glanced sideways at Randy. "Seems I can just manage a pie or two these days."

Andrew took the knife and cut the big pie into eight even pieces. No one said anything, for no words could do justice to Gran's cherry pie. After they had finished eating and were sitting around the fire, Benj looked up into the gathering twilight where a few stars were showing like sparks from the brush fires. "Thank you, Lord," he said in a deep, slow voice, "for making a heart and a pair of hands that can praise You with a pie like that."

After supper was finished, the young people got pails of water from the brook and soused the circles of ashes so there would be no danger of a spark blowing or the wind whipping flame into sleeping embers during the night. Then they gathered up their tools and started across the field. At the crest of the hill, Andrew and Peter and Benj said good-by to the others, who kept on across the field and went down to the valley while they turned toward the house.

On the doorstep, Benj stood still and reached into his pockets. One by one he produced the eight rattles and laid them in Peter's hands.

"For trust," he said solemnly.

"But, Benj, you did it all!"

The old man shook his head. "Only the cleaning out at the end, and that was not so important as the discovery you made at the beginning."

"Thanks, Benj," Peter said, a smile lighting up his face.

Rain came again that night, steadily, comfortingly. Andrew heard it and thought how right Benj had been to see that they got the brush burned when they did. Then he turned over and went to sleep and his dreams were of a herd of cows with red *A*'s on their backs grazing in pastures green as emeralds.

The next day was fair, and Benj spent much of it in the vegetable garden working up and down the rows, pleased to see how the crops had rallied after the drought. There would be plenty, he thought to himself, as there always was, enough for their needs, and then some.

Benj shared his thoughts with the mountains, lifting his eyes to the hills that rimmed his world and made it a good place for a man to grow. There were some people who felt that Benj had missed a great deal by spending most of his life in one place. When they said so to him he merely smiled and shook his head. The answer was in his heart though it did not find its way to his tongue, and it was that there was never so much need for a man to grow wide as it was for him to grow high.

Benj sighed in deep content and went to his afternoon's work in the barn. He saw Peter come from the house and go toward the garden. He saw Andrew walk down the lane toward the mailbox. The sun was shining on them all.

Shortly before it was time for the milking, Benj went in search of Andrew and found him in the kitchen. A letter was in his hands and such a smile was on his face as made Benj stand still in the doorway.

"Martha's coming home!" Benj exclaimed.

"She is," Andrew said, "and even sooner than I expected her. Tomorrow." He held the letter up so he could read from it to Benj.

Leonard has been not only on the mend but on the go these past two weeks, and I can see that it is safe for me to leave. The baby has a strong hold on life and young Ellen is a wonderful mother. I've done what I came here to do, but I did not think when I came that I'd be away for so long.

Andrew folded the letter and put it back in its envelope. "No more did I," he commented.

"She'll be coming in on that five o'clock train tomorrow evening?" Benj asked.

"Yes. That's what she says. I'll leave first thing in the afternoon and take a couple of crates of pullets. There's always a market for them and that will make the trip count both ways."

Benj turned to go back to his work, then he remembered what he had come to tell Andrew. "Buttercup Princess should be taken to Green Mead tomorrow if you want her bred this month."

"I do want her bred now, for I want her calf to be born in the early spring."

Benj stood silently, then he said, "I could lead her over myself, but I'd planned on going up to the sheep pasture tomorrow and start breaking Dusty in for the time when we bring the flock down."

"I can't fail Martha," Andrew said, his brow furrowing as he wondered how he could be in two places at once.

Benj's eyes twinkled. "This won't be the first time that a man's been caught between womenfolk."

Andrew was too concerned even to smile at Benj's remark.

"You were going to take Peter along with you when you went," Benj reminded Andrew. "Why don't you let him take the heifer by himself?"

Andrew shook his head. "Princess is too valuable to be in a boy's charge for a whole day."

"There's a time when a boy becomes a man," Benj spoke quietly, as if he were talking to himself. "Today you see him as a boy, and the next time you see him he's a man, and no one can say when the change has taken place."

Andrew looked down at the letter in his hands. Benj waited to hear what Andrew might ask him to do, but when no words were forthcoming he turned and started out of the room.

"Where is Peter?" Andrew called after him.

"In the garden."

"Tell him to come here, will you, Benj?"

Benj went out, a smile playing over his face. He moved slowly, not from his years but from a feeling that this was no time for haste. Whatever Andrew had in his mind to do, an extra minute or two to think about it would only aid him in the doing.

Peter was working down a row of onions, digging them out of the earth and turning them into neat piles to dry in the sun and the wind. The firm round onions shone in their golden skins, and Benj, standing at the edge of the garden and letting his eyes rest on them, felt the same thrill of pride that he did in all things coming out of the earth and, with the pride, a reverence at what was given to man if he put his hands in the soil and did his share of work.

Benj waited until Peter came to the end of a row then he said quietly, "Your father wants to see you, Peter, in the house."

"What about?"

"Maybe it's one thing, maybe it's another."

Peter looked back at his work, satisfied that the onions he had dug up were all exposed to the sun. He thrust his tool into the ground. His mind, at that moment, was less on his father than on the onions. He wanted Benj to admire this crop that was being dug.

"Perhaps they're not so big as other years," Peter said, "but they're fine and firm and even in size."

"Aye, it's a good crop and it will please your mother. She always said there was nothing like an onion to give body to a meal." Benj's eyes were shining with his secret. "Your father has some news for you, Peter."

"For me?" Then Peter knew that the light in Benj's eyes could mean only one thing. "It's Mother! She's coming home!"

"Aye, she'll soon be slicing some of these very onions into a stew."

Peter let out a shout and raced across the grass to the house. He arrived in the kitchen breathless and glowing, with the grime of the garden on his hands and the sweat of his labor on his face.

Andrew held the letter toward him. "Your mother is coming home tomorrow," he said.

"Tomorrow? Mother is coming home tomorrow?" Peter fairly shouted the words, joy ringing from every syllable.

Andrew beamed at his son and nodded his head as if the news was still so unbelievable that he would confirm it in every way he could. "I shall go to meet her train, but I had planned on taking Buttercup Princess to Green Mead tomorrow. If she doesn't go then she can't go for another three weeks, and I want her calf to be born in April before the heat of the summer." Andrew paused. "I had thought you and I would lead the heifer over your path, but now—"

Peter waited, wondering what his father would do. In his wonderment the smiles that had wreathed his face fell away, and he looked like a hot and dusty boy who was tired from doing a man's work in a garden.

"Now, I'm going to ask you to lead her over for me," Andrew said.

Peter felt a queer weak feeling come over him. "Me?" he asked, and his voice sounded as wobbly to him as his knees felt.

"Yes, you," Andrew said with emphasis.

"Do—do you think I can?"

"I know you can." There was assurance in Andrew's smile.

Peter stood quietly as Andrew told him what he must do. He inclined his head from time to time so Andrew would know that he heard, but his thoughts were racing through his mind so rapidly that he was not sure he heard everything.

Andrew said that he must lead the heifer slowly, never hurry her, let her stop to drink at the brook once or twice along the way, and give her some grazing if he found any grass. When he reached Green Mead Farm he was to turn her over to the herdsman, who would take charge of her. It might be for an hour or two that the herdsman would have her, Andrew could not say, but Peter could find some place during that time where he would not be in the way and could eat his luncheon.

"On the way home, before you get into the woods," Andrew said, "let Princess graze again. Let her take the journey back at her own pace. It should be possible for you to be home before dark. Princess may walk slowly but she won't drag too much for she'll be wanting the companionship of her own herd by then and the goodness of her own pasture. If all goes well with us," Andrew concluded, "your mother should be here by the time you get back."

Peter sighed and smiled. Any journey would seem short with that promise at the end.

"Do you understand all that you are to do?"

Peter nodded. He understood that his father was trusting him with his valued heifer.

"Good. I'm going out to do the milking now."

"Shall I come with you or finish the onions?"

"Finish what you've started. You'd best get the onions under cover before evening."

Benj had gone to the barn and Peter worked alone in the garden, brushing the dry earth off the onions, putting them in mesh bags that would be hung in the shed so they might go on curing.

Now the summer that had seemed so long and unmoving was rushing past on wings, Peter thought. Tomorrow Princess would go to Green Mead, and he was the one who would lead her over the new path through the woods. Tomorrow his mother was coming home. In only a few more tomorrows he would be going back to school. Summer was flying, flying. Peter heard a faint sound far overhead. Looking up he saw a wedge of wild geese heading south across the sky.

12 The New Peter

Andrew cooked a breakfast for Peter that he knew would carry the boy through the day. When they had finished, he pushed his chair back from the table and said, "We'll do your chores this morning, Peter. I want you to get going as soon as possible. Meet me in the barn when you're ready."

"All right, Father. I won't be long."

Peter went upstairs to make his bed, careful to draw the spread smooth and tight so that there would be no wrinkles showing, for his mother would soon be seeing it. In large red letters on a white sheet of paper he printed the word WELCOME and stood it on the dresser in his parents' room, then he raced down the stairs to the kitchen. He slapped a piece of cheese between two pieces of bread and wrapped it in his handkerchief, then stowed it in his pocket. He pulled on his stout boots and drew the laces tight; then he looked around the kitchen to see if there was anything that needed to be done before he left. His heart was tumbling over with joy. The next time he saw that familiar room his mother would be in it.

Slamming the door behind him, he ran across the grass to the barn with Dusty and Shep leaping around him, darting at his heels and barking in rollicking and contagious fun.

Andrew and Benj were standing in the barnyard with Buttercup Princess between them. The heifer wore a halter with a length of rope hanging from it. The sun was shining on her golden coat; her eyes looked brown and soft. Peter thrilled with pride at the sight of her, sure that in all the length and breadth of the countryside there was no cow so fine and handsome as his father's Buttercup Princess.

Benj put the rope gently into Peter's hand. "She'll show the boy how she wants to take it, Andrew. This is her day, and your day too." Benj's smile passed from father to son, then back to the patient heifer.

His father clapped Peter on the back and said jauntily, "Get on your way, Peter, and come back to a supper cooked as it should be by your mother's hands."

"Have an eye for porcupines," Benj warned. "They say there are more than a few around this year."

Andrew laughed. "First it's snakes and then it's porcupines!"

"Aye." The old man nodded. "Peter might as well have his eyes open for something along the way."

"Come on, Princess," Peter said.

The heifer moved into her stride, walking beside the boy, out of the barnyard, across the grass, into the field and toward the woods, where green shade looked alluring in the bright sunshine of the August morning. Peter could feel the eyes of the two men on him, but he did not look back.

It was pleasant walking along the path that had been cleared for this very purpose. The brook, running full since the recent rains, made a merry, friendly sound. The circles of blackened ash where the brush piles had stood were mute reminders of much that the summer had witnessed. In places, vines of wild grape hung in the trees, and the grapes that had looked hard and green for so long were now beginning to blush with blue. Stopping for a moment to let Princess drink, Peter climbed a tree and broke off a cluster that had more color than the rest. They were almost ripe, and Peter savored the tangy sweetness of the skins, but his mouth puckered at the tartness of the pulp.

Except for the wind in the trees above them and the running of the brook and the slight rustling made by hoofs and booted feet, there was no sound in the woods, and nowhere did the silence seem deeper than when they went over the shale. Peter paused and looked up at the rock ledges. He heard only stillness and saw only rock walls reflecting light.

Princess traveled willingly. When they reached the abandoned orchards of Green Mead Farm, she dragged on the rope a little for the first time. Putting her head back, her nostrils dilated as if she could smell the cidery apples that lay under the trees and would taste them for herself.

"Come along, Princess." Peter tugged at the rope. "You can have some apples on the way home, but we mustn't stop for anything now."

Reluctantly she moved away from the apples. They went through the old orchards, then along a lane skirting the new-bearing orchards and the open fields. At the entrance to one of the barns Peter met the herdsman.

"I've brought you Buttercup Princess," he said.

"I've been expecting you." The herdsman stood back and looked at the heifer appraisingly, then he walked slowly around her. "She's a beautiful animal. Your father has a right to be proud of her."

Peter handed him the lead rope.

"Make yourself at home, sonny. I'll take good care of the heifer. They'll give you some milk in the dairy when you're thirsty."

Peter wandered around the barns looking at the cows, then he went to the dairy where one of the men gave him all the milk he could drink. After a while he climbed into an empty wagon standing near a barn door, ate his sandwich and, having nothing better to do, went to sleep.

The voice of the herdsman woke him.

Peter blinked. "What time is it?" he asked, trying to stretch out of him the stiffness his cramped position had given him.

"Just gone three," the herdsman said.

"How is she?" Peter asked, scrambling down from the wagon to stand beside Buttercup Princess.

"Couldn't be better," the herdsman answered. "She'll have a nice little calf next spring."

Peter grasped the lead rope in his hand.

"Tell your father we'll send the registration papers along tomorrow. He gave me all the details about the heifer a while ago, but I've got to fill in our side of it. How far is it to your farm?"

"About an hour, taking it easily. I could do it in less time on my own, but it's slow going with a cow."

"Well, that's as it should be. Let her choose her pace. She'll lag at first, but once she knows she's headed for her own place, she'll pick up a little. Did you see any game in the old orchard when you came by?"

"No. What's there?"

"Almost anything is apt to be there these days. The apples have fallen and are rotting on the ground and they're tempting to most wild things. Rabbit and grouse are fairly common, but you might see a deer if you look sharp, and keep your eyes open for porcupines. There are plenty of them about."

"Do they like apples too?"

The herdsman nodded. "They come from the woods hunting for anything tasty, and when they find the apples they feast on them."

"Can I let Princess have some apples?"

"Sure thing." The herdsman laughed. "Cows can't seem to get enough of those cider apples. They'll clean up everything under a tree that has fallen in the night. They'll follow through a whole orchard or work right up a hillside of trees, and by the time they've finished you wouldn't find one of them able to walk a straight line!"

Peter's eyes widened. He wondered what his father would think of the stately Princess if she ate too many apples.

The herdsman gave the heifer a light slap on the rump. "Tell your father I'm coming over to see him one of these days. We're all interested in the herd he's developing."

"I'll tell him." Peter gave Princess a tug on the rope. "Good-by for now."

"Good-by, sonny. I'm glad our farms are so close together."

"So am I," Peter called over his shoulder, wishing he could run all the way back to his father's farm. For the first time that day he felt impatient at the heifer's slow pace.

Princess turned her head back to the barn. Peter pulled on the rope and started off. Reluctantly she followed him, ambling so slowly that Peter wondered if they would be home before the stars came out.

When they reached the old orchard, Peter turned the heifer loose, and while she searched for succulent grass, he climbed tree after tree in search of sound apples to take home with him. He filled his pockets and stuffed others down his shirt front, eating freely as he picked. His mother would like these apples with their hard skin and tart flesh, he thought, and she would like to know about the old orchard that was still bearing fruit, though it was given little care.

Glad for her freedom, Princess flicked her tail and tossed her head, making a few running steps between her mouthfuls of grass. Then she caught the spicy scent that had intrigued her on the way over. Ducking her head, she began nosing among the rotten apples at the base of the trees.

While Buttercup Princess worked under the trees, Peter climbed like a squirrel among limbs and branches until his pockets were full and his shirt front was bulging. From the edge of the woods he heard the sudden snort of a deer. Looking up quickly, he caught a glimpse of an antlered head and then the flash of a white flag as the deer disappeared into the woods again. Grouse were clucking, and distantly he heard the whirring of a pheasant. He began to feel as if he and the heifer were trespassers in a world that belonged to the creatures of the forest. He was aware of a slow swishing sound near the trunk of the tree among whose branches he was perched. Looking down, he saw the sleepy face of a middling-sized porcupine looking up at him.

Princess came nosing her way through the grass, and Peter, eager to ward her off from any encounter with a porcupine, scrambled hastily down the tree. The tree was so gnarled and spiky with dead wood that first his pants caught on a limb and had to be yanked free, and then the sleeve of his shirt; but he reached the heifer in time to grab the dangling lead rope and pull her away from the tree.

The porcupine lumbered clumsily up the tree Peter had vacated. Grunting and chattering, it looked down at the boy and the cow who had disputed its territory.

Peter leaned back against the heifer's solid flank and sighed with relief. He dared not think what his father might say if he had let a porcupine make a pin cushion of her nose.

"Come on, girl, we've got to make tracks out of here," he said, and Princess followed him willingly through the orchard and into the woods.

When they came to the brook, Peter gave the heifer her head and she dipped it low in the water, drinking deeply and then holding it for the water to run over her nose. Careful of the apples bobbling in his shirt, Peter knelt down beside the brook and put his lips to the water. He had not known how thirsty he was, or how hot. After they had both drunk and were refreshed, they went along the path together.

Dusk was beginning to settle in the woods, but the path was clear before them and wide enough for them to walk side by side. The brook was a friendly companion, whispering away and sometimes laughing in the silence. Even if twilight came down before he emerged onto his father's open fields, Peter had the comforting feeling that there would be a line of light above the path between the lines of foliage that bordered it. When his eyes could no longer trace the path on the ground, he would look up and follow the one marked on the sky.

Martha stepped down from the farm truck and let her eyes linger on the familiar scene, so well remembered, so deeply loved. All that she saw was bathed in the golden light of the late afternoon sun. Andrew ran the truck into the barn. Until he returned, Martha would not move.

Slowly her eyes traveled from the door of the house to the garden that looked well cared for and fruitful, to the barn with its complement of cows that had come in for the milking, to the fields that reached away from the farm buildings, the distant green of the woods. Once her circle was complete, she let her eyes return to the house and rest on the door again. She was eager to go through the waiting door and feel in her hands the clasp of the tools she loved to work with. But soon she would be pushing it open. Soon she would be standing in the quiet intimacy of her kitchen, surrounded by pots and pans, shiny stove and useful sink, things that knew her well and responded to her touch.

It was a small world, she thought, this perfect circle that her eyes had made, yet it held all that was most dear to her. Then she lifted her eyes to the mountains, not for the first time that afternoon but in delight that they were there, that they always had been there and always would be.

Shep came running from the barn, aware of Martha's arrival and eager to greet her. Dusty, bigger than his mother and a powerful dog though still full of gangling ways, trailed behind. With high sounds of joy, Shep leaped and barked in welcome. Dusty did the same, though he was not sure who it was that he was greeting. Martha reached out her hands and held Shep's head between them.

"Oh, Shep, you have so much to tell me," Martha said. "And what a fine son you have!"

Shep waved her tail. In her eyes was all that she had to say: the assurance of her love which neither time nor distance could change.

Andrew came up to Martha, picked up her bags and started to carry them into the house. Benj followed with a pail of milk, which he put down hastily when he reached Martha. She held out her hand to him, palm open and up as was her way. Benj closed his two hands over it. They looked into each other's eyes and searched each other's faces, as old friends will when they have not met for a space of time. As always, Benj saw in Martha's face a deeper kindness, and Martha saw in Benj's a deeper wisdom.

"Is the place looking as you thought it would?" Benj asked.

"It looks lovelier than I had ever remembered it, and yet somehow it looks just the same."

"The garden has done well in spite of the dryness, and the cows and the sheep are all right. It's that boy you'll be wondering about. He's grown like a young tree, straight and strong." Benj beamed. There were moments when he could not remember that Peter was not his, he took such pride in him.

"Oh, Benj, Andrew said he had sent him to Green Mead with Buttercup Princess. I'm so glad, but I hope he'll be back soon."

Benj glanced over his shoulder toward the field, expecting to see Peter leading Princess across the grass toward them.

Andrew joined them. "I knew he'd not be back before we were," he said, "but he'll be along soon now." Andrew turned and walked a few paces across the field to get a better view of the way that led into the woods.

Martha looked earnestly at Benj. "Has everything righted itself between those two?" she asked in a low voice.

"Aye, indeed it has."

Martha smiled with a deep happiness. "I sensed it in their letters. Oh, Benj," she sighed, "those two were born to work together, not to be at odds!"

Andrew returned and they all went into the house. Soon Martha had changed her clothes and commenced to prepare supper. Her hand turned to the familiar tasks as if she had not been away.

Benj brought a basket of newly dug potatoes to her. "First of the crop," he said.

Martha picked one up in her left hand, it was round and smooth. Her right hand closed around the handle of the paring knife, which was only a little more smooth.

However, she was not to get supper that night. Almost as soon as she had started her preparations, there was a knock at the door. Mary and her grandmother came in. Between them they carried a basket in which they had packed a complete supper for four people. Everything was there except a pot of coffee and that, Gran said, could be properly made only by Martha herself. There was laughter and exchange of talk between them all. Martha and Andrew urged them to stay and share the good things they had brought, but Gran was firm.

"That boy of yours has a man's appetite now and we won't be the ones to take the food out of his mouth by staying. We'll come again one day and eat your food, but not our own tonight, thank you."

"Has Peter grown so much then?" Martha asked, for until Peter himself came into the house she felt she could not ask enough questions about him.

Gran nodded her head. "And more than in inches."

After Mary and Gran had left, Martha turned to Andrew and asked him what Gran had meant.

"You'll see soon enough for yourself." Andrew smiled.

Benj opened the stove and put in more wood to get up heat for the coffee. "And why shouldn't Peter grow?" he asked. "There's something in the mountains that makes a man reach up when it's in him to respond."

Martha went to the window, but the view from it did not take in the open fields.

Andrew watched her. He knew how impatient she was to see their son. Ever since he had met her at the train and had seen the smiling expectancy in her face, the deep questioning in her eyes, he had known that something within her could be answered only by Peter himself. "How is Peter? Tell me about

Peter!" she had said more than once as they drove over the road through the valley and up the long hill to the farm.

"I'll go to meet him," Andrew said. "Perhaps that will hurry him along."

He went out of the house and walked quickly down the fields. Twilight filled the air and the woods were full of shadows. Standing where the green curtain of foliage hung, Andrew listened and peered into the shadows.

"Peter!" he called, breaking the silence of the woods. "Peter!"

Clear on the night air came the answer, "Father!" and then again, "Fa-ther!"

"Where are you?"

"Not far. Where are you?"

"Not far." The words traveled down the clearing like an echo.

Andrew started over the path in the direction of Peter's voice. Five minutes, a small portion of a mile, separated them. Andrew covered it more quickly than the boy with the cow, who picked her way carefully through the deepening dusk. They met, and Andrew saw Peter's face, a white oval against the darkness. In it was the confidence that comes to one who has carried out his trust.

"Everything go all right?" he asked.

"Oh, yes." Peter smiled. "It's been a wonderful day."

Andrew turned and they walked along together on either side of Buttercup Princess.

"Is Mother home?"

"Yes, she is, son. Home and waiting for you."

"It's getting dark, isn't it?" Peter commented, looking up into his father's face and thinking what a welcome blur of light it made.

"Have you had any trouble finding your way?"

Peter shook his head. "There's still light in the sky."

"Your mother is impatient to see you, Peter."

"How is she, Father? Does she look any different?"

"Not that I can see," Andrew said, "and she hasn't all the years I've known her." He paused, then he laughed softly. "Come to think of it, Peter, she does look different. She looks—well, taller."

"Taller?"

Andrew nodded. "I always thought her head was among the stars. Now I know it is."

Where the path emerged onto the open fields, Andrew took the lead rope from Peter's hand. "Why don't you go up and see for yourself, son? I'll look after the heifer."

Peter needed no persuading. "See you at the house," he called over his shoulder, as he started running up the hill.

Andrew stood still for a moment as he watched Peter's figure racing over the pasture slope. That was his son, Andrew said to himself, and the one who was his friend and partner.

Princess pushed her head against Andrew's back.

"I know, I know," he answered her gently, "you're as eager to get back as we all are." He started forward with slow, even steps on the dew-wet grass of the pasture.

Peter ran all the way to the door of the house, the apples he had gathered knocking together in his shirt front. There was a light in the kitchen, and he could see Martha bending over the table, putting something down, straightening up again.

"Mother!" he shouted. He pushed the door open and rushed in.

Martha looked up as Peter came into the room. For a minute they stood and looked at each other, each wondering if the other was the same, the familiar, the long known. Peter reached into his shirt front and took out the apples warm from their journey. He ranged them on the table, but he did not take his eyes from his mother. Then he came around the table toward her.

"It's you," he said. "Really you. And you're not any different. Father said you were the same."

She held out her arms and Peter found his old haven in them. But he was different, Martha had to admit as she raised her head to gaze into his eyes. When she had gone away she had looked down into his eyes; now their eyes were on a level. She held him at arm's length and looked up and down his strong rangy frame. Yes, she thought, it was what Benj had said: things happened that had done more than make Peter grow. They had turned him into a man: a man the mountain world had made.

She smiled and closed him in her arms again. She liked this new Peter, though it might take a little while to get to know him.